It *had* to be her. He had never seen anyone else with such incredible hair.

His gut tightened as his gaze zeroed in on the back of the woman with the riot of red tresses that fell like a stream of fire to her waist. Old memories, old hurts, old desires stirred within him. He took a moment to breathe deeply and acknowledge the fact that Francesca was really here, that he was close to her after so long. A combination of fate and planning had brought him back to Strathlochan.

And to Francesca Scott.

Luke allowed himself the luxury of savouring the sight of her. Even dressed in her unflattering uniform of white tunic and trousers she stood out, her five-foot-nine-inch height, shapely figure and eye-catching hair making her impressive and impossible to ignore. She was even more gorgeous than his imagination had suggested she would be. But ten years was a long time. The timid sixteen-year-old girl had matured into a stunning woman.

He ached to touch her, to find out how good she felt now.

But every thought went out of his head when she turned her head and looked at him. All he saw were those remarkable silver-grey eyes— eyes that for years had haunted his dreams and instantly made his insides slam with need. Eyes that widened now in stunned recognition.

'Luke?'

'Hello, Chessie.'

Dear Reader

I cannot believe that THE REBEL SURGEON'S PROPOSAL is my tenth Medical™ Romance for Mills & Boon, and my eighth set in and around my fictional world of Strathlochan in rural Scotland. It all began back in October 2006, when my first Medical, THE ITALIAN DOCTOR'S BRIDE, was published. One of the things I love so much about writing these loosely linked stories is never saying a final goodbye to characters I have come to love so much. Each book stands alone, but I hope the feeling of community and interconnected lives is something that you enjoy as a reader, too.

It is now the turn of Strathlochan Hospital's diagnostic radiographer, Francesca Scott, to step out from the shadows. We also meet Luke Devlin, the man who hopes to make her future very different.

Luke and Francesca come from very different backgrounds but they gravitated together growing up...both loners, both having problems at home, both on the outside looking in. Theirs was an unusual friendship, but important to them both. Until they were parted as teenagers ten years ago.

A chance meeting begins this story, sparking a chain of events which brings the past crashing back. Now a surgeon, Luke has a promising career ahead of him—but what matters most is claiming Francesca, and he'll do whatever is necessary to achieve his goal.

Next in line to tell their stories will be Rico and Ruth and Gus and Holly. I hope you will come along for the ride as these dedicated and caring medical professionals face up to their private fears and personal issues, finding love and happiness in Strathlochan.

Love

Margaret

THE REBEL SURGEON'S PROPOSAL

BY
MARGARET McDONAGH

MILLS & BOON

All the characters in this book have no existence outside
the imagination of the author, and have no relation
whatever to anyone bearing the same name or names.
They are not even distantly inspired by any individual
known or unknown to the author, and all the incidents
are pure invention.

First published in Great Britain 2009
Large Print edition 2009
Harlequin Mills & Boon Limited,
Eton House, 18-24 Paradise Road,
Richmond, Surrey TW9 1SR

© Margaret McDonagh 2009

ISBN: 978 0 263 20551 0

Set in Times Roman 16½ on 18¼ pt.
17-1209-54398

Harlequin Mills & Boon policy is to use papers that are
natural, renewable and recyclable products and made
from wood grown in sustainable forests. The logging and
manufacturing process conform to the legal environmental
regulations of the country of origin.

Printed and bound in Great Britain
by CPI Antony Rowe, Chippenham, Wiltshire

Margaret McDonagh says of herself: 'I began losing myself in the magical world of books from a very young age, and I always knew that I had to write, pursuing the dream for over twenty years, often with cussed stubbornness in the face of rejection letters! Despite having numerous romance novellas, short stories and serials published, the news that my first "proper book" had been accepted by Harlequin Mills & Boon for their Medical™ Romance line brought indescribable joy! I love developing new characters, getting to know them and setting them challenges to overcome. The hardest part is saying goodbye to them, because they become so real to me. And I always fall in love with my heroes! Writing and reading books, keeping in touch with friends, watching sport and meeting the demands of my four-legged companions keeps me well occupied. I hope you enjoy reading this book as much as I loved writing it.'

www.margaretmcdonagh.com
margaret.mcdonagh@yahoo.co.uk

Praise for Medical™ Romance author Margaret McDonagh:

'This is such a beautiful, wonderfully told and poignant story that I truly didn't want it to end. Margaret McDonagh is an exceptional writer of romantic fiction, and with VIRGIN MIDWIFE, PLAYBOY DOCTOR she will tug at your heartstrings, make you cry, and leave you breathless!'
—*The Pink Heart Society Reviews*

'Romance does not get any better than this! Margaret McDonagh is a writer readers can always count on to deliver a story that's poignant, emotional and spellbinding, and AN ITALIAN AFFAIR is no exception!'
—*CataRomance.com*

ACKNOWLEDGEMENTS

Special thanks to all the following,
who have given me so much support and
encouragement, kindness and care…

Jo, Anne, Richard, Chris, Sue H, Liz,
Lorraine, Pam, Maggie, Sue S, Sandy,
Gwen, Gill, Sue R, Fiona, Lesley,
Jennifer, Jackie, Irene and Christine

You are all appreciated beyond words

CHAPTER ONE

February

'FRANCESCA? My goodness, lass, is that you?'

After responding to a call from the A and E department to carry out a series of emergency X-rays on a road-accident victim, Francesca Scott was returning to the radiology unit when she heard someone call her name. Glancing round, she saw an older woman sitting in a wheelchair at one side of the reception area, separate from the handful of other people who were awaiting attention. Recognition dawned as Francesca observed the plump figure, her gaze travelling over a rounded face framed by short grey curls. A familiar face that was kindly and surprisingly unlined by the ravages of a difficult life…a face that now bore the signs of bruises that had Francesca's stomach twisting into knots and suspicion sending warning bells ringing in her mind.

Old memories flowed, fast and furious, nearly overwhelming her, making her feel hesitant, vulnerable, taking her back to the girl she had been ten years ago rather than the woman she had since fought to become. Part of her wanted to run, to push the myriad of scary emotions away, but she could never turn her back on the woman who had recognised her and reached out to her. Feeling as if she was crossing some unbridgable chasm to an unknown destination rather than a few feet of floor space, Francesca closed the distance separating them. As she sat on a chair beside the woman, she studied the bruising and noted the way she was cradling her right arm in a sling.

'Hello, Mrs Devlin.'

A smile bloomed, bringing a twinkle to faded green eyes that displayed pleasure and warmth, making her look much younger than her sixty-three years. 'It's wonderful to see you, Francesca!'

'Thank you. And you. I wouldn't have wanted you to be here under these circumstances, though.' Trying to keep barriers erected against anything personal, or anything related to the past, Francesca focused on Sadie Devlin's injuries and why she had been left alone. 'Have you been seen, or are you waiting for an X-ray?'

'I'm not sure what's happening. The nurse who brought me here from Casualty went off to talk to a friend and hasn't come back. She's a bit of a flighty one.' The admission was made with a mix of wry amusement and a hint of frustration.

Francesca cursed under her breath, pretty sure who the culprit was. 'Do you know her name?'

'Olivia, I think. Dyed blonde hair, lots of make-up.'

It figured. She tried to hide her annoyance at wretched Olivia Barr, who had no doubt gone off after some man who had caught her fancy. 'Is that the X-ray request form?' she asked, gesturing to the slip the older woman held in her lap.

'Yes, that's right. Shall I give it to you?'

'Please.' Francesca stood up. 'I'll find out what's going on and get you booked in.'

Mrs Devlin's relief was obvious. 'Thanks, lass.'

A quick check at the reception desk with Kim, one of the unit's clerks, confirmed that Olivia had failed to organise the requested X-rays and had left her charge unattended for some time.

After a hectic morning in Radiology, things were beginning to wind down, but as her colleagues on duty were all busy with patients who had pre-booked appointments, Francesca offered to handle Sadie Devlin's case herself.

'I thought you were on your lunch-break now?' Kim fretted as she wrote up the necessary paperwork and entered the details on the computer.

'It's OK.' Francesca was determined to ensure that Mrs Devlin did not have to wait another moment before she was made comfortable. 'I'm no longer on call for A and E and I'll still have time for a quick snack before I start on the appointments I have scheduled for this afternoon.'

The younger girl smiled as she handed over the file. 'Thanks, Francesca. I was getting a bit worried, especially when Olivia disappeared and just left the lady there. Things have been so busy I haven't had a minute, but I was going to speak to her if Olivia didn't come back soon.'

Making a mental note to have words with the tardy nurse, Francesca returned to Mrs Devlin and wheeled her to a vacant X-ray room.

'I'm not jumping the queue, am I?' the thoughtful lady fretted.

'Not at all. I'm just sorry you had to wait this long.'

Francesca prepared things in readiness to take the required images. As she turned to face the woman once more, dread filled her, a lump forming in her throat as she wondered how to voice her concerns about how she had been hurt.

'What happened today, Mrs Devlin? Did you have an accident or…?' Her words trailed off and she cursed the tinge of colour that warmed her pale cheeks, betraying her discomfort and, no doubt, making the direction of her thoughts all too clear.

Mrs Devlin sent her an understanding smile as the unspoken question hung in the air between them. 'It's all right, Francesca. Really. Yours is a natural assumption to make, after all. But on this occasion it was all my own fault. I climbed onto a chair to change a lightbulb. So silly of me.' She sighed, shaking her head. 'It was more rickety than I thought, and when it gave way, I overbalanced. The next moment I was on the floor. Instinct had me putting my hand out to save myself. I knew right away that my arm was broken.'

'Did you hit your head at all?'

'No, but I grazed my face on the chair as I

fell…hence the bruises. The nice doctor in Casualty was very thorough checking me over and my arm seems to be the only worry.'

'That's good news.' She smiled, relieved there was nothing more serious going on. 'Let's get these X-rays taken, then.'

'Francesca…'

A change in the tone of voice alerted her and she looked up, seeing both determination and the shadows of past pain in the older woman's green eyes. 'Yes?'

'Mick, my husband, died five years ago.' The announcement was delivered after a short pause and without emotion, but a welter of meaning resonated in those seven words.

Francesca bit her lip, unsure what to say. She couldn't express sorrow for the loss of a man who had been brutal and cruel, at whose hands Mrs Devlin and her three children had suffered for years and whose often violent crimes had led to several spells in prison.

The woman reached out with her uninjured hand to pat Francesca's arm. 'You don't have to say anything, lass. I know what people thought of him—of us as a family. Many wondered why I stayed, but it was for the children. I couldn't abandon them and Mick would never have let me take them away from him. My being there gave them some protection.'

Only at the expense of her own, Francesca wanted to protest, but held her tongue. She was angry on Mrs Devlin's behalf, she always had been, but even through the impotence of youthful rage, she had also long admired her courage and her love for her children. Not that all of them had deserved her selflessness. It was true that everyone in Strathlochan had known the history of the Devlin family and had spoken of them—the men, at least—with disgust and wariness. Rumours and prejudices had been rife about them and Francesca had grown up fearing Mr Devlin and the two older boys, Jon and Pete, who had shown all the signs of following in their father's unsavoury footsteps.

Her own home life had been nothing to write home about but for all the problems surrounding the Devlins, Francesca had always envied them Sadie. Her care for her children had been obvious, even for Jon and Pete, who had repaid her dedication so shabbily. To Francesca, Sadie Devlin was all a mother should be…the kind of mother she herself had always longed for. So many times growing up she had admired her from afar, had played make-believe in her mind, pretending Sadie *was* her mother and that someone loved her for herself, always had a kind word for her, a ready hug. Reality had always intruded—a reality without the love and cuddles and kind words she had so craved.

Pushing aside unwanted memories, thoughts of things she had long since tried to banish and shut away in a dark, secret part of her mind, Francesca focused on her task, being as gentle as she could as she positioned the injured arm so she could capture the clearest picture of the suspected fracture. Explaining exactly what she was doing and ensuring her patient was as comfortable as possible, Francesca retreated to the protected cubicle while the X-ray was taken.

'I need to take one more picture from another angle and then we'll be finished,' she explained, returning to the main room. 'I'll be as careful as I can.' Even so, Mrs Devlin winced as her arm was moved and repositioned. 'I'm sorry.'

'Don't worry, lass, it has to be done.'

Francesca worked swiftly to minimise any discomfort and, once she had completed the X-rays, resettled Mrs Devlin's arm in the supportive sling. The images were soon ready to send to the A and E department but there was still no sign of Olivia Barr. Angry that the nurse had deserted her patient, Francesca decided to return Mrs Devlin to Casualty herself.

'How long have you been back in Strathlochan, lass?'

The question caught Francesca by surprise, once more reawakening things she wished to keep dormant and in permanent hibernation. 'Nearly three years now,' she confided as she guided the wheelchair down the maze of corridors that were so familiar to her but could easily confuse the unwary.

'And you like it here at the hospital?' Sadie probed.

'I do. I love my job.'

Saying the words out loud confirmed the truth of them. For the first time in her life she felt she fitted somewhere, Francesca admitted. She relished the variety of the work she did, both within the radiological unit itself and when she was on call to A and E. The buzz and uncertainty of the emergency work appealed to her, being quite different from the order and organisation of the unit and set appointments.

As a rule, she wasn't good with people, but she enjoyed the interaction with her patients, devoting herself to their care and doing her best for them while they were in her charge. Outside her professional life, once she shed her work persona, she avoided people as much as possible. She knew that her nickname around the hospital was the Ice Maiden but it didn't bother her. The people who dubbed her that knew nothing about her or her life. She got on all right with most of her colleagues in the work environment, but any kind of social interaction made her uncomfortable.

She had a few people she counted as friends. One was A and E doctor Annie Webster, who was currently recovering from a frightening incident when she had been attacked while on duty three weeks ago, an assault that had nearly killed her. It had been a scary time and still made Francesca shiver when she thought of it. She had been on call in A and E when the assault had occurred and had done the ultrasound scan that had shown the flooding of blood into Annie's pericardium from the stab wound to her heart.

Annie was now home and making a good recovery from the emergency thoracotomy that had saved her life. Francesca had been to visit her friend several times and, in the process, she was getting to know Annie's fiancé, Nathan Shepherd, another trauma doctor who had recently come to Strathlochan to be with Annie. Theirs was a romantic story—not that Francesca had much time for romance. Not for herself, anyway. But she was very glad Annie was happy.

Francesca thought of the few other friends she had allowed into her life since her return to Strathlochan, including married doctors Cameron Kincaid and Ginger O'Neill, who ran the local Ackerman Centre for self-harm and eating disorders. Then there were nurse Gina McNaught and her Italian fiancé, Dr Seb Adriani, now working at the town's new multi-purpose drop-in centre, and Frazer and Callie McInnes, both connected to Strathlochan's air ambulance. Callie was a paramedic, but she had given up her flying role now she was pregnant, while flight doctor Frazer was considering returning to a hospital-based job when the baby was born.

Generally, though, she preferred animals to people, Francesca acknowledged. Animals didn't let you down, didn't judge you, didn't lie or deceive.

'It was a shock to discover you and your mother had left Strathlochan. We had no clue where you had gone,' Sadie continued, startling Francesca from her wayward thoughts and surprising her even more that her absence had been noted at all. 'And I'm so glad I've seen you today, lass. I had no idea you were home.'

Home. Francesca was relieved that she was behind the older woman so Sadie could not see her reaction to that word. She didn't want to think of home, of childhood and all that meant. Once she had finished school after her Highers exams and had been old enough to make her own decisions, she had packed up and gone, deaf to the inducements, threats and promises of change. She'd ended up in Edinburgh where she had done her four-year training to be a diagnostic radiographer, a career that appealed to her interest in science and technology and, through her sporting activity, in anatomy and physiology.

Coming back to Strathlochan to take this job had been an act of defiance as much as anything else. It had been something she had felt she had to do and to face, even if no one but her understood the significance of it or knew of her inner struggle. She had carved out a good life here, had faced the demons and the memories, had moved on and was more settled than she had ever imagined she could be. The job provided constant variety and gave her independence to make decisions. Unlike some of her colleagues, she didn't even mind the night shifts...indeed, she enjoyed them. Especially given the way the forward-thinking Trust ran Strathlochan's hospital and medical services.

The local health board's innovative management was one of the things that had impressed her so much when she had taken the job back here. Thought had been given to improving working conditions for doctors, nurses and other clinicians. While they still worked hard, and for long hours, their shifts had been changed from the old-style patterns still in place in many hospitals. In Strathlochan most now worked a rotation of five days on, two days off, three nights on and three days off. It had worked well and the majority of staff appreciated the schedule. It not only improved general quality of life, but it had created good teamwork and aided patient care.

Arriving back in the A and E department, Francesca checked Sadie back in at Reception and asked to speak to the doctor in charge of her case. She was relieved to discover it was Nathan Shepherd, not only because she felt comfortable working with him but because she knew his reputation for looking after his patients was fantastic. Sadie was in the best of hands. She gave Nathan the X-ray images, which showed a clean, straightforward Colles' fracture of the radius near the wrist, a common injury and one which, in Sadie's case, showed no displacement or angulation and which would need no manipulation. She also took a moment to inform him of Olivia Barr's dereliction of duty.

From the anger and resignation in Nathan's dark eyes, she didn't imagine he was surprised at the news. 'I'll take care of it, Francesca,' he promised, and she knew the transgression would not go unpunished.

'How's Annie doing?'

A rare smile softened his handsome face. 'She's getting better every day. Thanks for asking. Are you coming round to see her again soon?'

'I'll pop in on my way home after work,' she promised. 'I have my days off next week before starting a night shift so I'll ask her if she'd like to have lunch then.'

'Annie will be delighted. She always loves seeing you—you're a great friend.'

Francesca gave a nod and stepped back, both warmed and yet unsettled by Nathan's words, still edgy at the very concept of friendship and being emotionally close to people, even those she liked as much as she did Annie. 'I'll just say goodbye to Mrs Devlin, then I have to get back to the unit.'

'Is she special to you?' Nathan queried with evident interest.

'I grew up here in Strathlochan.' She paused, unsure what to say, how much to explain. 'She was good to me when I was young.'

'I'll take care of her.'

Grateful for his understanding, she went to see her charge settled in the cubicle where Nathan would discuss her fracture and explain what was to be done. Francesca lingered a moment longer, feeling the pull of the past and stirrings of her childhood affection for this woman.

'Are you going to be all right?' A frown of concern creased her brow. The nature of her job meant she usually had only a brief connection with each patient, but she always did her best for those in her care. 'Will you be able to get home?'

'My next-door neighbour brought me in and is waiting for me.'

Partially reassured, Francesca smiled. 'And will you be able to manage while your arm is in plaster? Is there anything I can do to help? Any shopping you need picked up?' The offer was out before she could retract it, but the woman was shaking her head, her eyes twinkling with amusement.

'It's kind of you to worry about me, lass, and I much appreciate your thoughtfulness. But as soon as Luke hears what I have done he'll be insisting I go to stay with him so he can take care of me. That boy would wrap me in cotton wool given half a chance,' Mrs Devlin confided with a laugh.

Luke.

Francesca closed her eyes. Her heart lurched and she suddenly found it hard to breathe. Luke…the youngest son. So different from his scary, no-good father and bullying, troublesome brothers. Just hearing his name brought an overwhelming welter of emotions. To say she'd not thought of Luke in ages would be a lie. He had invaded her thoughts and her dreams with worrying regularity during the last decade. Seeing his mother again had opened up thoughts and feelings she had long tried to lock away because there was too much pain and longing and confusion. Luke, who had left town ten years ago when he had been eighteen. They'd had an unusual friendship. Nothing more. Yet she had built Luke up in her lonely teenage mind as her hero, had looked to him as her protector. Which was why her sixteen-year-old heart had been so broken, and why she had felt so betrayed when he had gone without a word, without so much as a backwards glance.

Unsettled by the tidal wave of disturbing memories, she said a hasty goodbye to Sadie, wishing her a speedy recovery. And then she fled. She didn't want to think about Luke. Not after all this time. But however much she tried to fool herself to the contrary, she had never forgotten him. He was in her head far too frequently, a hazy shadow on the edge of her consciousness, giving her no rest.

Francesca squared her shoulders and gave herself a stern talking to as she walked back to the radiology unit, any thought of a hasty lunch forgotten in the need to bury herself in work to block out old hurts and disturbing memories.

She had been nothing to Luke. He hadn't even

known she had existed and had likely never thought about her again after he had left town. Growing up and forgetting all about him was long overdue.

Luke Devlin was in the past...and that was where he was going to stay.

The phone was ringing as Luke Devlin let himself into his soulless London flat. It was situated on the second floor of a small, purpose-built block on a noisy street within walking distance of the hospital where he worked...a street jammed with traffic and people and where the buildings crowded together, pressing in on him. It made him feel claustrophobic and long for the wide-open spaces and clean air of his home town of Strathlochan in Scotland.

Even after a decade he hadn't really settled in London. He'd lived in this flat for four years and still didn't know his neighbours. And, as much as he enjoyed his work and got along well with his colleagues on a professional level, he had few friends socially. Once a loner, always a loner. Or was the stigma of his name and his background so ingrained in him that he subconsciously put up barriers and kept people at a distance?

Dog tired, he cursed under his breath as the phone continued its insistent ring. He knew he had to answer it. But if it was one of the orthopaedic team calling him back to the hospital, he was not going to be pleased. He'd been up for a stupid number of hours and all he could think about was a hot shower before falling into bed. He was too exhausted to even bother to eat. Shrugging off his well-worn leather jacket and leaving it draped haphazardly over the back of the sofa, he flopped into an armchair, picked up the cordless handset and barked his name.

'Devlin.'

'Hello, love. You sound grumpy and worn out. Has it been a tough day?'

'No more than usual, Ma.' A smile came unbidden in response to the familiar voice. God, he missed her. The one constant in his life. 'How are you?' A too-long pause had his instincts on red alert. 'Ma? What's happened?'

The answering chuckle eased some of his tension. 'I have good news and bad news.'

'Tell me the bad news first.' Leaning back in the chair and stretching his legs out, he tried to relax muscles that were stiff and aching after long hours standing at the operating table, assisting his boss in complicated spinal surgery.

'Don't be cross with me, Luke, I'm absolutely fine,' his mother began, immediately warning him that she was far from all right. 'I had a little accident and broke my arm.'

'Ma!'

She tutted soothingly. 'Now, then, don't take on, Luke. The nice doctor at Strathlochan Hospital told me that it's a clean and simple break and it should heal without problems.'

'What did you do?' Shaking his head, he listened to his mother's confession, knowing there was no point in reprimanding her for acting so foolishly. 'Are you in pain?'

'It *was* very sore but I have some pills and I'm much more comfortable now it's in plaster,' she reassured him.

His weary brain rallied, thoughts and questions rushing at him. 'Which doctor did you see?' Meticulous at work but not the tidiest of people at home, he had to rummage through the clutter on the table near his chair to find a pad and pen.

He jotted down the name Nathan Shepherd, planning on ringing straight away to get the full information first hand and, if possible, to ask to see a copy of the X-ray. As a specialist ortho-paedic registrar, bones were his life, and he wanted to satisfy himself that all was well with his mother's arm.

'How are you going to manage at home alone, Ma?' he asked, voicing his concerns.

Despite a strong effort on his part, she refused to allow him to return to Scotland to collect her. Not that he had anticipated anything else. But a few moments later, and with suspiciously little argument, he *did* persuade her to come down to London on the train and stay with him for a while. He'd be much happier having her close so he could keep an eye on her progress. Her agreement had been too easy, however, and he was wary. He knew his mother. She was up to something.

'You said there was good news, as well,' he reminded her, allowing himself the luxury of relaxing again.

'I did. And there is! You'll never guess who took my X-rays.'

Luke rolled his eyes as his mother, ever the one for spinning out a good yarn, paused for effect. 'I hope this person was kind to you.'

'Oh, she was *wonderful*,' his mother gushed,

clearly smitten. Luke hid a groan, hoping this was not part of another unsubtle and completely pointless matchmaking plan. He was grateful, however, to the unknown woman who had apparently shown his mother such care, a fact she now confirmed as she related the tale of being abandoned by the unprofessional nurse and the subsequent rescue by the radiographer. 'She was very gentle and very kind, and she looked after me so well.'

'And what is the name of this paragon?' he asked, knowing his mother would persist until he gave in and deciding to get it over with.

'Francesca Scott.'

Luke forgot how to breathe. A knot tightened in his chest and it felt as if his heart had stopped beating altogether before it resumed pumping at a rapid rate. Somehow he sucked a ragged breath into parched lungs. Gripping the phone so hard his knuckles were stark white, he sat up straight in the chair, every part of him at full attention.

'What did you say?' He demanded clarification, knowing he must have been wrong, must have been hearing things.

'It's true, Luke.' His mother's voice softened with the confirmation, filling with awareness of the importance of her words. 'Apparently Francesca has been working at the hospital for nearly three years. I had no idea. After seeing her, I made a few discreet enquiries. I didn't learn much but there are one or two things you might be interested to hear.'

He was interested, all right, although it took a few moments for the rest of the information to register over the roaring in his ears and the rushing of blood through his veins. One vital fact took precedence. Francesca was back. Scattered images and memories of long ago fired through his brain almost too fast for him to catch hold of them. Francesca as a coltish young girl, courageous and loyal. Friendless, just like him. Alone, just like him. Hurting and trying so desperately not to show it…just like him. So much in common, so much silent, mutual understanding, yet a chasm as wide as an ocean had yawned between their lives and their backgrounds.

His father had not wanted him to continue his education but even then Luke had stood up to him, knowing what he wanted and that his brain was his ticket out, the key to his future. It had paid off. The last violent row had happened the day he had finished his final Advanced Higher exam. He'd been eighteen, forced to leave home, to escape his father—needing, too, to follow his dream to be a doctor and prove himself.

Leaving his mother had been an impossible wrench, with the added worry of what might happen to her when he was not there to protect her, but she had been adamant he go, as selfless as ever. Battered and bruised, he'd slipped away like a thief in the night to lick his wounds. Then he had worked hard to establish a place at medical school in London, doing extra jobs to pay his way and finding somewhere to live so that his mother could come to him—as she had, living in London until his father had died and it had been safe for her to return home.

And then there had been Francesca. He'd felt bad leaving her behind but she had been just sixteen, tied to her home and shackled by her own problems. There had been nothing he could do. Not then. But he had never forgotten. Three years later, unable to get her out of his head, needing to know what had become of her, he had gone back for her, but she and her mother had vanished. After several unsuccessful attempts to find her, he had begun to give up hope of seeing her again.

Until now.

Because Francesca was back. And, as the information his mother imparted sank in, seeds were sown…seeds that immediately took root, germinated and began to grow with a life of their own. He had no idea what Francesca's life was like now, what she would say when she saw him again—hell, he didn't even know if she remembered him, if he had been any more than a blip on her consciousness a decade ago. But an inner demon possessed him and he couldn't let it go. Couldn't let *her* go. Not without knowing, once and for all.

It was crazy to act so spontaneously, to jeopardise all he had built here, but he knew what he had to do and nothing or no one was going to stop him. His boss, Professor James Fielding-Smythe, renowned orthopaedic surgeon, brilliant, impatient and demanding, would have a fit when he found out, but Luke didn't care. Whatever scathing criticism and shameless cajoling came from the crusty old professor, Luke was not going to be diverted.

Not now Fate had tipped his hand.

Not now he knew that Francesca was in Strathlochan.

Not now he had a plan.

CHAPTER TWO

8 weeks later—April

IT *HAD* to be her. He had never seen anyone else with such incredible hair.

Luke stared at the four figures walking ahead of him down the hospital corridor, two male and two female. But only one held his attention. His gut tightened as his gaze zeroed in on the back of the woman with the riot of red tresses restrained in a thick plait that fell like a stream of fire to her waist. Old memories, old hurts, old desires stirred within him. He took a moment to breathe deeply and acknowledge the fact that Francesca was really here, that he was close to her after so long.

It had taken eight weeks and had necessitated turning his life upside down to get here, incurring the ire of Professor James Fielding-Smythe when no threats or inducements could persuade him to change his mind about leaving. To be fair, once he had known he was defeated, the prof had given in—if not entirely gracefully. His reference had been glowing, however, and his backing invaluable in rapidly securing Luke's new job.

But even with his goal firmly in mind, Luke had experienced some uncertainty about coming back to Strathlochan. This was the town where he had known so much strife and unhappiness as a child, where he had been judged and labelled, ostracised as a teenager, written off because of the reputation of his father and his older brothers. Damned from birth because he carried the Devlin name. Yet he had felt stifled in London, had missed his home environment, the freedom of the forests and the hills. And, he acknowledged, a part of him still felt the need to prove himself, to show the bastards they couldn't beat him, that they had been wrong about him. To prove that he was worth something, that he *was* different from the rest of the men in the Devlin family.

A combination of fate and planning had brought him back to Strathlochan. And to Francesca Scott. Whilst he would never wish any harm to befall the mother he loved and respected beyond measure, the accident that had led to her broken arm had turned out to be fortuitous. Lady Luck was shining on him for once in his life. A slow smile curved his mouth as he watched Francesca's rear view, the natural sway of her hips, unintentionally provocative and classically feminine. His mother had not exaggerated when she had said that the coltish girl had grown into a beautiful woman, fulfilling the promise that had always been there through her youth.

Francesca…

Whilst he remained unobserved, Luke allowed himself the luxury of savouring the sight of her. Even dressed in her unflattering uniform of white tunic and trousers, she stood out, her five-foot-nine-inch height, shapely figure and eye-catching hair making her impressive and impossible to ignore. He enjoyed another leisurely perusal, from the sweep of her slender back, over the appealing curve of her bottom and down long, athletically graceful legs. A runner's legs. Legs he had always dreamed would wrap around him as he sank deep inside her silken heat. He never had. Not yet. But he would. Even when times had been at their most desperate and finding her again had seemed impossible, he had always known he was destined to claim her, that he and Francesca were meant to be together.

The group stopped at a junction in the corridor and, as Francesca half turned to talk to her colleagues, Luke could see the swell of lush, ripe breasts under her fitted tunic. A fresh lick of desire ran through him, tightening his gut. She was even more gorgeous than his imagination had suggested she would be. But ten years was a long time. The timid sixteen-year-old girl had matured into a stunning woman.

As he slowly closed the distance between them, he absorbed her perfect bone structure, the curve of her jaw, the sensuous mouth, the creamy skin that had been as soft and velvety as a peach. He ached to touch her, to find out how good she felt now. Then there was that hair…the thick and lustrous rich red corkscrew curls. One hundred per cent natural and unique, just like the rest of her. Let loose, those curls would cascade around her shoulders and down her back like living flames. His fingers itched to bury themselves in the silken, fiery mass, to have the strands caressing his skin, to see them fanned out across his pillows.

Francesca had always been a lady—and way out of his league. She appeared as graceful and stylish ten years on, enough that just looking at her reminded him of the chasm that had yawned between them. The classy girl who, outwardly, had appeared to have everything and the boy from the wrong side of the tracks with the bad reputation. Flickers of anger and doubt churned in his gut. What made him think he had any more right to be around her now than he had a decade ago? Yes, he had changed. He'd beaten his background, his father's legacy, and had made a success of himself, had shown he was his own man. Had Francesca changed, too? If she remembered him at all, would she view him as she once had or would she now regard him in the same way the rest of the town had always looked on a Devlin male…as something dirty to be wiped off the undersides of their shoes?

He needed to look into her eyes, to know what lurked there now, to see if the sadness and innocence had gone, to judge her expression as she faced him unprepared. As he neared her, she frowned at whatever was being discussed. He sensed her tension, her discomfort in the presence of her colleagues, noting the way she moved back to maintain her personal space. At once he felt protective, ready to step in if needed, just as he had all those years ago when he had put himself between her and the bullies at school.

But every thought went out of his mind when she turned her head and looked at him. All he saw were those remarkable silver-grey eyes—eyes that for years had haunted his dreams and instantly made his insides slam with need. Eyes that widened now in stunned recognition.

'Luke?'

His name was a whisper of breath on her lips. He stood still under her swift observation of him, aware of the curious glances of her colleagues. Her gaze skimmed his face and clashed with his own once more.

'Hello, Chessie.'

'My God, it *is* you.' Shocking him with her unexpected boldness, she stepped forward and slid her arms around him in a welcoming hug he had never dreamed she would initiate. That his surprise appearance had knocked her so off balance that she acted this out of character took his breath away. 'It's been years.'

Ten long, solitary years. Instinctively his arms

closed around her, drawing her as tightly against him as he dared without alarming her. One hand splayed across the small of her back, tempted by the enticing swell of her rear, while the other hand indulged in feeling the silken strands of hair bound now in the braid—a braid he wanted to knot around his wrist so he could draw back her head and plunder her mouth with his own. He somehow managed to resist both urges to touch and to taste.

What he couldn't resist was to nuzzle into her to breathe in her very essence. Her subtle scent, flowery and sensual, teased his nostrils, sparking his desire anew, reminding him of the one other time in his life he had been able to hold her this close for far too short a time. Then she had been a girl, now he felt the woman…all soft curves and feminine sweetness. The seductive press of firm, perfect breasts against his chest that made him want nothing more than to bare them, shape them, taste them, bury his face against them. Francesca belonged in his arms, in his bed. And if all went to plan—if dreams really did come true—she would be there. Soon.

With regret, he allowed her retreat as soon as he sensed her withdrawal. She stepped back a pace, failing to mask her confusion at her effusive welcome of him, uncertainty evident in the slightly slanted mesmerising grey eyes fringed by long, thick, sooty lashes. The young Francesca would have been too shy and scared to approach anyone, much less have physical contact with them. He could tell from her growing tension that the reticence to touch and be touched outside a professional setting remained, and that her initial, instinctive response to him had shocked her. All of which confirmed that deep inside Francesca hadn't changed that much and that he needed to be gentle and patient with her.

Luke watched the play of emotions across her face as she pulled herself together. The scattering of freckles he remembered so well dusted the ivory skin across her high cheekbones and over her small, straight nose…freckles that had always intrigued him. He longed to know where else on her body she had them, wanted to kiss each and every one.

Her lips held his attention next. Unadorned and dusky pink, they were the perfect shape, the top lip with its Cupid's bow and the sensual curve of the fuller lower lip. A mouth that was made for kissing, a mouth he yearned to taste. He searched her eyes, relieved to see in those silvery depths a memory of the girl she had been. A hint of the innocence was there, the aloneness, as was the acceptance of him for who he was, and he was thankful the years had not hardened her or coloured her view of him.

Now he needed to spend time with her, to learn about the woman she had become, to begin to draw her back in to him. 'Are you in a rush? Do you have some time to talk?'

He knew she was free because he had found out her schedule and planned his business at the hospital to ensure that he saw her. But would she admit it or would she try to fob him off? The outcome was crucial and uncharacteristic nervousness fluttered inside him as he waited for her answer.

'I'm on my lunch-break.' Her smile, tentative though it was, warmed him from the inside out, but it was her ready agreement that pleased him most. He waited as she turned to excuse herself from the colleagues who were still hovering nearby. 'Is it all right if we talk about this later?'

'If we must, Francesca.' The lukewarm comment

came from one of the men, his gaze speculative and not entirely friendly as he looked at Luke.

Luke returned the appraisal coolly, issuing a silent warning of his own, wondering if the guy had designs on the lady himself. Tough. Now he had found her again, he wasn't making way for any other man to make a move on her. Stepping closer to her side, he settled a proprietorial hand at the small of Francesca's back, feeling the jolt spear through him as the connection was made. He steered her down the top-floor corridor in the direction of the staff canteen before anyone could detain them or she could change her mind.

Francesca could not believe Luke was here, in the flesh, as if she had conjured him up from her dreams. Dreams that had plagued her in the past eight weeks since she had seen his mother. Eight weeks in which she had been unable to get Luke out of her mind, despite telling herself countless times that she had to forget about him. She had never expected to see him again but here he was, very much a man in place of the boy he had been ten years ago, but even more seductive, wicked and drop-dead gorgeous than she remembered.

Six feet three inches of solid, leanly muscled male. Dressed in dark grey chinos and a shirt a couple of shades lighter, he looked smart but casual, definitely not a man anyone would ignore. The top button was undone, the open collar displaying the strong column of his throat, while the shirt's sleeves were rolled up to the elbow, revealing foreams lightly dusted with golden hair. His hands were well shaped and attractive, the nails neat and cared for—and one of those hands remained on her back, branding her skin through the thin fabric of her tunic. A ripple of awareness ran along her spine, centring on that touch, on the closeness of his body as he walked beside her, brushing against her with every step. She could feel his warmth, detect the earthy, musky aroma of him that teased and excited her senses. What was wrong with her? She never reacted like this, and certainly never noticed the way a man smelled, for goodness' sake!

Her pulse racing, her body burning, she cast a furtive glance at Luke from the corner of her eye. Collar-length dark blond hair, shot through with lighter strands, framed a strong, far-too-handsome face, a seductive mouth that promised sin and those startling green eyes, watchful, intent and clever, but gleaming with devilment. Oh…there was little doubt that the bad boy still lurked within Luke Devlin! She had only just seen him again after a gap of ten years, yet she could tell that there was so much more behind the relaxed outward image he portrayed. Anyone who wrote him off as some kind of lazy surfer character would be in for a surprise—ignore the sharp intelligence at your peril.

She had yet to recover from the shock of acting so out of character that she had boldly stepped up and hugged him. It was as if some inner compulsion had taken her over, driving her to do something she would never normally do. Whatever had possessed her? She didn't touch people. Not voluntarily, personally, not beyond what was necessary for work. And she hated to be touched. Yet her first instinct had been to embrace Luke. Brazenly. She had initiated the contact, had enjoyed it, had not wanted to let him go. She had been drawn to him rather than holding herself apart, excited rather than repelled, aroused rather than turned off. Being in Luke's arms had felt *right*. And that scared her.

Francesca very much feared that however

much she had tried to convince herself to the contrary over the years, she had never got Luke out of her head…or her heart. But there had never been a future for them beyond her foolish imagination. If Luke had ever been aware of her at all, it could only have been as the annoying girl who had hung around on the periphery—always on the outside, looking in.

For years growing up she had watched Luke from afar but they had come from such different worlds. Her own, materially rich but emotionally poor, had been strict and repressed, governed and controlled by her domineering mother, while Luke's had been rough and wild, coloured by the Devlin reputation, his father and older brothers always in trouble with the law. Not that she had ever believed the things they had said about Luke. He'd been nothing like the other Devlin men. Luke had never been anything but kind to her, as protective as an older brother, her hero, her secret love, until he had vanished ten years ago.

Francesca realised with despair that she was even more attracted to Luke now than when she had been a shy, awkward teenager. A shiver of remembered embarrassment ran through her as she recalled the day the bullies had shoved her at him in the playground, daring her to kiss him. She would never forget Luke's kindness, his understanding. Or the unexpected, wildly exciting passion as he had given her her first ever kiss, a kiss she had never forgotten to this day. A kiss by which she had judged every one she had received since…finding them all lacking.

Her gaze slid from the green fire in Luke's eyes to the sultry curve of his lips. How would they feel now? What would the kiss of the man be like compared to the kiss of the boy? She smothered a gasp of shock as the very thought caused her breasts to swell with arousal. Her nipples peaked as she imagined the heat of his mouth on her flesh, his hands touching her all over, and a coil of fire tightened her womb and pooled between her legs. Dear heaven! This was *crazy*.

Shocked by her thoughts and her body's instinctive, betraying reaction, she allowed Luke to open the door for her and she stepped ahead of him into the canteen, both regretful and thankful when the disturbing touch of his hand dropped from her back. After selecting their food—a tuna salad for her and lasagne for him—they headed to a free table. Francesca was aware of the curious glances from fellow staff members and could imagine some of what they were thinking, seeing her with a man like Luke. She knew what they called her, and why, but, then, she had spent her whole life having people talk behind her back and call her names. Except Luke. For all their differences, the opposing reasons why it was so, they had shared that understanding, that empathy. Of being the outsider, alone, unwanted.

'Am I imagining it or are people staring at us?' Luke asked, the relaxed ease with which he sat down in contrast with the tight edge to his voice.

'No. People are probably shocked to see me here with you.'

Luke's expression hardened. 'Because I'm a Devlin?'

'Of course not,' she corrected him, displaying a hint of the inner steel it had been necessary for her to develop long ago to survive. 'I doubt they would even know, Luke, much less care. It's not you, it's me.'

'Why would that be?'

Francesca found herself captured by the expression in his magnetic green eyes—protective, sultry, intense. As if he was interested in her and what she had to say. As if she mattered. Clearing her throat of the sudden lump that seemed to have lodged there, and trying to clear her mind of her foolish fancies, she focused on her lunch as she answered his question.

'I'm known as the Ice Maiden around here.'

She had strived for a self-mocking tone, one that would signify that she didn't care a scrap what anyone said about her. That she hadn't quite pulled it off was obvious from the tiny pulse along Luke's tensed jawline and the narrowing of green eyes that flared with annoyance and the same kind of defensive gleam she remembered from their schooldays when he had been her self-appointed guardian.

'Are you, now?' He took a forkful of food, his gaze straying round the room, the challenge in them unmistakable to anyone who looked at him. 'I doubt they'll be calling you that much longer.'

It felt good to know that Luke's instinctive reaction was still to take her side without question. But she was an adult now, used to fighting her own battles. Besides, he was just visiting, passing through. She couldn't allow herself to get used to seeing him again, or to come to rely on him being her buffer against the difficult and hurtful things that sometimes happened.

No matter how hard she tried, she couldn't stop looking at him, searching out all that was familiar, learning all the changes maturity had brought to his far-too-handsome features. The dark blond hair was streaked by natural highlights and the sun. A couple of stray locks tumbled in reckless disarray across his forehead, adding to his rakish appeal. His face was masculine, strong, compelling, his nose straight, his cheeks lean, his clean-shaven jaw determined. She forced herself not to linger any longer on the temptation of his mouth, disturbed that she, who was always so cool and so uninterested in men, felt such a buzz of sexual awareness whenever she was near Luke.

The next moment she was looking into mesmerising green eyes, eyes that held a hint of mischief that stole her breath and a darkly sensual intent that shocked her and made her tingle all over. All manner of questions chased one another through her mind. Why was Luke in Strathlochan? What coincidence had brought them together in the hospital corridor at that moment in time? Where had he been these last ten years? What had he done with his life? Was he single? The last crashed her back to reality and fired a warning through her. It was no business of hers what he did and who he was with. Luke was a forbidden fantasy from her past. That was all. It would be wise for her to remember that rather than let her imagination, and this surprise meeting, run away with her.

'How is your mother, Luke?' she asked, seeking safer territory as they finished their meal. 'I saw her recently when she came in after breaking her arm.'

'I know, and I've been wanting to thank you. Ma told me how wonderful you were with her.'

His genuine gratitude, and his obvious care for his mother, warmed her. 'I was pleased to help. Has she recovered now?'

'She had the cast off two weeks ago and is fine. She came down to stay with me in London for a while but was glad to get back home.' He pushed his empty plate aside and leaned forward, resting his forearms on the table, the action somehow making him feel much closer. Green eyes watched her intently. 'It was thanks to Ma that I knew you were back in Strathlochan.'

'I see.'

Francesca didn't see at all. The remains of her lunch forgotten, she struggled to draw air into lungs that suddenly seemed compressed, and her heart thudded beneath her ribs as she tried to make sense of Luke's words. She wasn't aware he had ever known she had left Strathlochan and she found it hard to believe he had thought of her at all these last ten years. Conscious that her hands were shaking, she hid them under the table, clasping them in her lap, not at all sure what was going on here. And why couldn't she break the spell Luke seemed to hold over her? Despite being in a room crowded with people and filled with noisy chatter, being with Luke felt incredibly intimate, everyone and everything else fading to the background.

'So, have you been in London since you left town?' she asked, struggling for a nonchalance she was far from feeling.

'Yeah. I worked the first weeks at a hotel which had the benefit of giving me a roof over my head and food in my belly.' The quick smile was wry and did curious things to her insides.

'I'd applied to several medical schools and was delighted to get the results I needed in my Advanced Highers to take up the place I really wanted.'

The import of his words sank in. 'You're a doctor. That's great.'

'You're not surprised?' he asked, his expression curiously blank.

'Why would I be?'

This time the smile had a harder edge and no humour. 'I'm a Devlin, remember? We never amount to much.'

'Don't say that, Luke.' Her protest was swift, her anger rising that people who knew nothing about him could pass judgement, but also that he should ever believe the ignorant gossips. She managed to resist the urge to reach out to him, instead clenching the hand that had moved so instinctively into a fist on top of the table. 'You were the brightest, cleverest person I knew, not to mention the most thoughtful. And you worked hard. You were never going to be like them, were always going to make something of your life.'

One eyebrow, several shades darker than his hair, rose questioningly. 'You thought that?'

'Of course.'

'I wish I'd had the same belief!' His teasing faded, the expression in his watchful green eyes sober once more. 'You were always different, weren't you, Chessie? And I don't mean that,' he interjected as she stiffened involuntarily, accurately judging her train of thought, knowing of her past when she had been growing up. He moved, one fingertip resting lightly on the back of her tensed hand. Even that simple touch scalded her skin. 'I mean, in the way you saw me as a human being rather than an extension of a bad family,' he clarified, his finger brushing softly back and forth, sending a tremor right through her. Green eyes turned darker with an emotion she couldn't identify and his voice was serious and almost wistful when he spoke again. 'I've never forgotten the faith and trust you always granted me, or the way you stood up for me.'

Francesca had no idea what to say. She wanted to remove her hand from his caress and her gaze from his, but her body refused to obey her. 'Are you here to see your mother?' she asked as, shaken, she struggled to gather her composure, keen to put away the emotional memories yet unable to resist the temptation to discover more about the man he was now.

'That's one benefit of it.'

The cryptic response roused her interest but also made her edgy and left her feeling there was more he had to tell her, something important she had yet to grasp. 'One benefit of what?' she whispered, all too conscious that she sounded less like the confident, independent woman she had become and more the breathless, tongue-tied teenager of old.

For the longest moment, the very air seemed to still as she waited for Luke's answer. His hand enclosed hers, warm and strong yet exquisitely gentle as he linked their fingers together. Francesca thought she might go up in flames, not only from the contact but from the smouldering way he looked at her—as if no one else mattered, as if he saw her alone. Finally, he spoke.

'Fate. Timing. Three vital things falling into place at once. One was Ma. One was the job…'

Again Luke paused, and a shiver rippled through her at the seductive, intimate expression in his magnetic green eyes. As the tension and the electric charge between them continued to grow, she forced herself to ask the question now drumming inside her.

'What job?'

'As specialist surgical registrar on Maurice Goodwin's orthopaedic team.'

Francesca smothered a gasp of shock as Luke delivered the unexpected news. Her breath hitched and her heart rate kicked up with a mix of excitement and alarm as the full implications of what he had just said sank in. 'Here...in Strathlochan?' she clarified, scarcely aware that her fingers had tightened around his in response, as if seeking reassurance or grounding herself in reality.

'Here.' His voice, low and husky, spread warmth right through her. 'I'm home for good, Chessie.'

CHAPTER THREE

'How did it go?'

The question greeted Luke the moment he stepped through the back doorway into his mother's kitchen. 'OK. Good.' Two insufficient words to describe the events that had unfolded in the last few hours.

'Did you see Francesca?'

'Yes.' Typical Ma, getting right to the heart of things. Luke smiled to himself, watching as she bustled around, switching on the kettle to make tea and taking a tray of her legendary, heavenly scented almond shortbread from the oven and tipping the slab out onto a rack. 'We had a quick lunch in the hospital canteen.'

'And?' she persisted, turning to face him, eagerness and curiosity evident in green eyes that were a couple of shades duller than his own.

Luke pulled out a stool and sat at the breakfast bar, not at all sure how to put his thoughts and emotions into words. So he started with a simple fact. 'Francesca's even lovelier than you said.'

'The promise was always there as a girl and she's matured into a beautiful woman,' his mother stated, cutting the cooling shortbread into slices.

'That she has.'

His mother chuckled. 'I thought you would notice! How did she take your news?'

'There was no surprise that I'm a doctor—it seems that Francesca always believed in me,' he confided, still moved by her faith in him. 'Just like you.'

'Even very young she had a fierce streak of loyalty towards you.' She poured the tea, set a mug in front of him and then sat down, stirring a spoonful of sugar into her own drink. 'What about the rest of it…you being back in Strathlochan and working at the hospital?'

'That *did* surprise her.'

In fact, there had been a whole range of emotions in Francesca's expressive grey eyes when she had learned of his return. The surprise had been obvious, followed by a flash of excitement, a wash of pleasure and then a hint of alarm that had alerted him to the task that lay ahead of him. Winning her completely in the way he wanted could not be taken for granted.

'Does she know the reasons why you came back?'

'Not all of them.' He paused, succumbing to temptation and helping himself to a piece of still-warm shortbread that melted on his tongue, filling his mouth with buttery sweetness and the subtle flavour of almonds. 'Francesca needs time, Ma. We both do. It's been ten years. We need to get to know each other again.'

His mother nodded her agreement. Luke knew she had been aware what Francesca had meant to him all those years ago and how he had felt, especially when she had left town so unexpectedly and he'd not been able to find her. Now she regarded him, her expression curious. 'But you felt it? When you saw her again?'

Oh, yeah, he'd felt it! Luke shook his head, remembering his instant reaction to her, a reaction that had intensified the longer he had spent with her, listening to her, being close to her. 'It's still there—for me. The question is whether Chessie can come to feel the same.'

'There was always a special connection

between you, not that either of you understood it then. You were too young. But I could see it, and I held out hope, sure that Francesca was the right girl for you,' she admitted with a reminiscent smile. 'Who knows what would have happened had events been different and you hadn't been driven apart before your friendship had the opportunity to cement? It may have been too soon then, for both of you. Now you have a second chance.' She laid a hand on his arm, her tone cautionary. 'Take care, Luke. I know Francesca isn't that shy sixteen-year-old any more but for all her feisty exterior and façade of self-confidence, I sense she has a lot of inner scars. Don't forget her background.'

'I won't, Ma.'

Luke took the warning seriously. Having already recongised how spooked Francesca could become and how deeply her past was ingrained in her, he had no intention of rushing things. Their lunch together had passed all too quickly but even in the short time he had sat with her in the canteen, he had noted her discomfort when people had looked at them and she had been the centre of attention. He thought of the way she had told him of her nickname, the false bravado she had portrayed as she had pretended she didn't care what her colleagues said. But he knew she did. It angered him that people judged her without knowing anything about her. He planned to change all that—as he planned a lot of things now he was back and had found her again—but he would have to be patient. Not a trait he was known for, but where Francesca was concerned, it was worth it.

Whilst he had wanted nothing more than to publicly stake his claim to Francesca, he had reluctantly released her hand as they had left their table and exited the canteen, not wanting to make her the object of hospital gossip which would only unsettle her and set his own cause back. Having dropped the bombshell about his permanent return to Strathlochan, he had escorted a near-speechless Francesca back to the ground-floor radiology unit on the pretext of having a look around.

After his quick tour of the unit before the afternoon appointments had begun, he had been even more excited about his new job and the prospect of working with Francesca—of seeing her every day and edging back into her life. It had been a big risk, giving up everything to come here, and, whilst their reunion had gone well so far, he wasn't stupid enough to think things were going to be easy.

He'd met some of the other radiology staff, being careful to respect Francesca's feelings and keep things professional. And then, all too soon, it had been time to leave, but not before he had managed to extract her agreement to meet up with him after work. He couldn't wait. All he could think about was Francesca. Seeing her again had rocked him. She was beautiful and smart. But he sensed her aloneness—recognised it because he shared it. They were two of kind. Always had been. Now he had the most crucial challenge of his life ahead of him…to convince Francesca they belonged together. To encourage her to let down her protective guard and instinctive resistance.

The time ticked slowly by and, despite enjoying his mother's company, he just wanted to return to the hospital to meet Francesca at the end of her shift. What was she doing now? Had she found out yet about the talk he had enjoyed with her immediate superior, Dee Miller, and the request he had made? What was she thinking?

Luke looked at his watch, his impatience growing. Soon he would see Francesca again. He needed to spend more time with her, to find answers to the endless questions he had about her life these last ten years and, importantly, to discover just how much her past affected her present thoughts and behaviour.

The first part of the plan that had been born eight weeks ago when he had discovered Francesca was back in Strathlochan had been achieved. He had re-established contact, confirmed his feelings and had persuaded Francesca to see him. The next step was to rekindle their friendship…a friendship he hoped would lead to much more.

Francesca glanced at the clock as she hung up the telephone, relieved to see there was only half an hour of her shift left to go. Time yet to deal with the unbooked patient Kim had just asked her to see, sent through from the A and E department for an ultrasound scan.

All her scheduled appointments had been completed and for once everything had run like clockwork with no problems, interruptions or delays. And yet the afternoon seemed to have dragged by.

Even though she had been busy with a full list of patients requiring X-rays and ultrasound scans for a wide variety of injuries and illnesses, and had worked with her usual diligence and care, there had only been one thing on her mind.

One *person*.

Luke.

A timid knock on the door had Francesca trying to banish the image of Luke's sexy green eyes and sinful mouth from her mind. 'Come in,' she called, forcing herself to concentrate on the task at hand as a large woman with short blonde hair and scared blue eyes entered the room.

'The clerk at Reception sent me straight through,' she explained, her nervousness evident in the shakiness of her voice.

'That's fine.' Francesca smiled, trying to set the woman at ease. 'Please, do sit down.'

The woman took the chair opposite and handed over the file she was carrying. 'The doctor in Casualty said to give you this.'

Glancing at the request form, Francesca noted that Mrs Bryson had been seen in A and E by junior doctor Gus Buchanan who was querying the possibility of gallstones. Hence the requirement for the scan. Also noted on the sheet was

Mrs Bryson's anxiety. Francesca went through the usual introductory process she used with every patient, greeting them and telling them her name and her role, confirming their identity and that the details had been entered properly on the computer notes. Next she asked them to outline the reason for their visit and found out their history and if they had ever had X-rays or scans in the past.

'Have you had an ultrasound before?' The woman shook her head, clearly alarmed at what was to happen, so Francesca was swift to reassure her. 'It's a quick and painless procedure—just the same as pregnant women have to check on their unborn babies. The scan uses sound waves to see inside the body and build up a picture of organs and structures. In your case Dr Buchanan wants to check to see if you have any stones in your gall bladder that could be causing your symptoms. Did he explain that to you?'

'Y-yes,' Mrs Bryson stammered.

'OK.' Rising to her feet, Francesca crossed to the examination table by the ultrasound machine and made it ready. 'If you'd care to lie down for me… '

The woman hesitated. 'Do I have to get undressed?' she asked, betraying the source of her anxiety.

'No, I just need access to your abdomen, so we can adjust the clothes you are wearing.' Keeping businesslike but friendly, hoping to aid the stressed lady to relax, Francesca helped her to settle on the table. 'If you could lie more on your left side… That's perfect,' she praised, helping adjust the woman's clothing to expose the area she needed on the right side and across her abdomen while retaining as much of her dignity as possible. 'Now, I'm just going to put some gel on your skin. It's cold, I'm afraid, but it's necessary to get a good image.'

What she refrained from saying, so as not to upset Mrs Bryson any further, was that the larger the patient, the less sharp the image the scan could produce, given the layers the sound waves had to pass through. The woman was already self-conscious enough. 'Next, I'm going to run the hand-held transducer over the area and we'll see what we can find. You'll feel a little pressure as I get the best connection possible. It shouldn't cause you any discomfort, but tell me if you have any worries or there is anything you want to ask.'

With her patient declining the invitation to

look at the screen, Francesca began the scan. Although the image was not the sharpest, it was obvious at once that Mrs Bryson *did* have gall-stones. Several of them were apparent. She printed out copies of the images for the file, as well as saving the scan digitally for the doctors to review on screen, sending it through to A and E for Gus Buchanan. That done, she helped wipe the remains of the gel from Mrs Bryson's skin, clearing up while the woman adjusted her clothes and climbed off the table.

'Is that all there is to it?'

'To the scan, yes.' Francesca smiled sympathetically, hoping that the doctors could treat the stones without resorting to an operation, which she feared would scare the nervous woman even more. She jotted a few notes and handed the file back. 'If you'd like to take this back to the A and E department, Dr Buchanan will explain the results and discuss them with you. Always speak up and ask any of us questions if there are things you don't understand.'

'Thank you. You've been so kind.'

'My pleasure.' Francesca opened the door and showed her out, ensuring she knew her way back to A and E. 'Good luck, Mrs Bryson.'

Having finished her notes for the on-duty consultant radiologist who would review the day's cases and write any reports needed for the referring departments or GPs, Francesca tidied the room, relieved that no more unexpected patients arrived. It was time to go home. Time to see Luke. A curl of heat percolated inside her. Aware, too, of a mix of excitement and confusion, she headed for the women's locker room to change out of her uniform. Mindful of hygiene and the dangers of superbugs and cross-infection, one of several initiatives the hospital board had introduced was reinstating the policy of changing and laundering on site rather than allowing staff to wear uniforms to travel to and from work.

Only Dee Miller was in the room as Francesca entered. Her immediate superior, the head radiographer and technician was in her early fifties, short and plump, with warm hazel eyes and a dark brown bob. A lively, organised and caring woman, Dee had been working in the unit for many years. Well respected, she was responsible for the section Francesca worked in and for reporting to Derek Barwick, the chief consultant and clinical director of the radiology department.

'Everything all right?' Dee asked, already dressed in street clothes and in the process of putting her discarded uniform into the hospital laundry basket before returning to her locker, a few down from Francesca's.

'Fine, thanks.' Detecting an odd note in Dee's voice, she looked at her colleague and frowned. 'Why? Have I done something wrong?'

'Goodness, of course not!' Dee reassured her with a surprised laugh. 'You're the best radiographer we have. No, I just thought you seemed distracted this afternoon.'

Francesca shook her head, unable to explain that she had been in shock since meeting up with Luke at lunch time. Instead, she hid behind her locker door on the pretence of rummaging inside for her things.

'The new surgical registrar made quite an impression,' Dee continued, a teasing note in her voice.

Feeling a blush warm her face, Francesca kept her head buried in her locker. 'Mmm,' she murmured noncommittally.

'I gather you know each other.'

'We went to the same school as children,' Francesca allowed, downplaying the connection even though she feared Dee was not going to let the subject drop. 'I've not seen Luke for ten years.'

'For once it seems all the talk about changes in the orthopaedic department and rumours of a high-flying new surgeon coming here were true.' Dee closed her locker door and sat down on the bench, clearly settling herself in for a good chat. 'I heard that Maurice Goodwin snapped Luke up after he was left a man short on his team when the last registrar, Adrian Lomax, left under a cloud after that botched operation.'

Like everyone else, Francesca had heard the talk, but she seldom paid much attention to hospital rumour. With Dee confirming that the news about the new surgeon was true…and that it referred to Luke…she knew that he had trained in London under the renowned ortho-paedic maestro Professor James Fielding-Smythe.

'Luke must be an amazing young surgeon if the brilliant but curmudgeonly old professor fought so hard to keep him and gave him such a glowing reference.'

Dee's words confirmed Francesca's own thoughts and she felt a flash of pride at Luke's achievements. 'I'm not surprised. Luke was always bright and hard-working,' she allowed, removing her tunic and trousers before pulling on her jeans and fleece top.

'Some people are commenting about Luke being one of the town's notorious Devlins,' Dee remarked, stirring Francesca's temper and protective instincts.

'They have no right to judge him! Luke is nothing like his no-good father was, or his older brothers.' She struggled to hide her emotion. 'Luke and his mother suffered much at Mick Devlin's hands.'

Dee nodded, satisfaction evident in her voice. 'I'm glad to hear you speak up for him, Francesca. I don't like rumour and careless talk any more than you do. And it makes my decision both easy and right,' she added, causing Francesca to frown in confusion as she sat down to lace up her trainers.

'What decision?'

'I've made some changes to the schedule and I've moved you to cover the fracture clinic tomorrow. Is that OK?'

'Sure,' Francesca agreed, used to working in different sections of the department. All the staff rotated duties to keep their skills up to date and prevent themselves becoming stale, and Francesca enjoyed the variety. 'I don't mind at all.'

Dee's smile widened. 'Excellent. Because I was talking to Luke earlier, when he looked round the unit, and he specifically asked if he could work with you.'

'He did?' This time Francesca could not disguise her blush, or her surprise that Luke had done such a thing. 'I wonder why.' Tying the laces on the second trainer, she sat back, puzzled. 'Maybe he just wants someone he already knows on his first day at work.'

'You think so?'

Francesca glanced round at the scepticism in Dee's voice. 'I don't know what else it could be.'

'Don't you? I'm sure Luke will enlighten you soon enough.' The older woman chuckled, as if privy to some secret Francesca had yet to unravel. Rising to her feet and picking up her bag, Dee headed towards the door. 'See you tomorrow, doll.'

Confused, Francesca watched her leave, thankful that no one else had been in the room to witness the strange conversation. Immediately her thoughts returned to Luke, where they had been ever since she had bumped into him so unexpectedly in the hospital corridor. She still couldn't believe that he was back in Strathlochan. For good, he had said.

After lunch, Francesca had felt nervous and self-conscious introducing Luke to some of her colleagues—soon to be *his* colleagues—wondering what they would think at seeing them together. But no one had said anything, and Luke had been professional and courteous. Even so, Francesca had remained conscious of the awareness and tension that simmered between them. Dee had happily agreed to Luke's request to familiarise himself with the radiology unit and, showing him around, Francesca had been impressed with his interest and knowledge.

By the very nature of their jobs, the orthopaedic and radiology departments worked closely together and they shared a wing on the ground floor of the hospital. The realisation that she was going to be seeing a lot of Luke in the days and weeks ahead had occupied much of her attention all afternoon. As had the knowledge that she had somehow found herself agreeing to meet him when her shift ended. There was much for them to talk about, he'd told her. She had not stopped wondering what he had meant. And she also wanted to know the other reason he had come home. Upstairs in the canteen he had said there had been three things that had brought him home. His mother, the job and…what? She couldn't explain why, but Francesca felt jittery and fizzing with nerves.

Seeing him again had been amazing, rousing all manner of exciting and scary feelings inside her, but the knowledge that it wasn't a one-off, that he wasn't passing through, that he was back, supposedly for good, and that they would be working together had really thrown her for a loop. Part of her was wary, uncertain. Another part of her welcomed his return with open arms. Even with the ten-year gap, and her sixteen-year-old self's inner sense of betrayal at his abrupt departure, she felt close to him, comfortable with him, as if it had been yesterday they had last spoken and not a decade ago.

Despite the new friendships she had formed over the three years since her return to Strathlochan, in particular with Annie, Ginger, Callie, Gina and their partners, she always held part of herself back and felt a certain distance from them. Luke was the only person with whom she had ever felt natural and understood. She welcomed the opportunity of experiencing that again. But the sexual chemistry, her aware-ness of him and desire for him, were scary com-plications she could do without.

She didn't do trust, didn't do commitment, didn't do intimacy, and she had long ago learned not to need or want anyone, to depend on no one but herself. There had only ever been one person in her life she had allowed herself to trust, one person who had ever seen her for the person she was inside...until he had vanished from her life, leaving her truly alone. Luke Devlin. Now he was back, as suddenly as he had gone, and a tor-menting voice nagged at her that he could dis-appear again just as easily.

Francesca glanced at her watch, feeling a prickle of fearful excitement and confusion— she was due to meet him in five minutes. Her heart in her mouth, feeling every throb of her racing pulse, she stood up, closed her locker, hooked the strap of her canvas bag over her shoulder and left the room. Reaction set in, the knowledge of where she was going turning her legs to rubber and making every step closer to Luke seem a dangerous act of folly.

Walking along the corridor, she caught sight of her reflection in a large glass partition. She had never been a girly girl, had never fussed with fashion or make-up, but she suddenly wished she was wearing something more appealing and feminine than her warm fleece top in battleship grey and her faded jeans with the frayed rip across one thigh. Her thick plait, untidy after a day at work, hung down her back. All at once she felt like the awkward teenager of ten years ago, the one who had never fitted in and who had always felt alone.

As she headed towards the main entrance, she had no more time to think or worry because all she could see and focus on was Luke, standing inside the doorway. A small package held in one hand, he had a smile on his face as he chatted to Donald Orr, one of the hospital's longest-serving and most popular security men. Her steps faltered as she took in the sight of Luke. He'd added a leather jacket to the outfit he'd worn earlier, giving him even more of the masculine, bad-boy air that was so appealing and exciting. Experiencing a strange fluttering inside her, she took a shaky breath and began to close the gap between them.

* * *

'A fine woman, your mother,' Donald Orr commented with sincerity and affection. 'Salt of the earth.'

That the security guard was one of those in the town who had always been supportive filled Luke with appreciation. 'She certainly is.'

'And now you're to be joining us here at the hospital.' The rugged, balding man beamed a gap-toothed smile as he shook his hand. 'Right proud your mother was when you qualified as a doctor. She must be delighted to have you home.'

'It's good to be back.'

And not only to be closer to his mother, who wasn't getting any younger, Luke allowed, a prickle at the back of his neck alerting him to the presence of the main reason for his return to Strathlochan. He turned his head, watching as Francesca crossed the broad foyer of the hospital's main entrance towards him. The ever-present spark of desire flared within him as he studied the way her faded jeans hugged those long, shapely legs. They should be illegal, he decided, noting the ragged rip in the soft denim across one thigh, which allowed a tantalising glimpse of pale skin with each step she took. The grey fleece top was loose and masked her figure, but its colour enhanced the mesmerising shade of her eyes.

Not wanting to be rude, Luke murmured a hasty farewell to Donald, then stepped forward to greet Francesca as she approached. A rush of emotion swept through him as he looked at her, appreciating her understated, natural beauty. Aware of where they were, and of her sensibilities, he didn't touch her, as he yearned to do, but he was close enough to be teased by her subtle flowery fragrance.

'Hi.' She halted, glancing around nervously before looking up at him.

'Hi,' he replied, seeing the confusion in her eyes, the mix of pleasure and anxiety. Also the weariness. 'You look tired… Busy afternoon?'

She fell into step with him as they headed out of the door, both of them waving to Donald, who smiled and gave them a thumbs-up in response. 'There was a full list of appointments, plus some extras sent through from A and E. How about you?'

'After completing all the hospital formalities of the paperwork, getting my ID and so on, I had a meeting with Maurice Goodwin and met some of the team. Then I spent some time with Ma before coming back to meet you.'

Having discovered that Francesca came to work by bike, he had walked back to the hospital from his mother's, carrying with him the bag of goodies she had sent. They reached the covered bicycle shed and he waited for her to unlock the security tag. She refused his offer to wheel the bike, so he walked beside her as they crossed the expanse of the car park, out onto the street and turned down the hill towards the town. The April day had been warm, but the sun had disappeared in the late afternoon and there was a chill in the air. Now they were away from the hospital, he edged closer, taking her free hand in his, linking their fingers, relieved when she didn't pull away.

Even the simplest of touches fired his blood but he marshalled his self-control. Wanting her to feel relaxed and at ease in his company, he kept things impersonal and they talked about inconsequential things. Francesca's voice was like a physical caress along his nerve endings. He could listen to her all day. Her voice was feminine with a low smoky tone that complemented the soft burr of her Scottish accent—an accent he himself hadn't lost after ten years away. He wanted to spend all the time with her he could, to take her out for a nice dinner, but he knew she was tired, on top of which he was wary of moving too fast too soon and scaring her off.

'Would you like to pick up a pizza or something?' he asked instead.

'Sure. That would be good.'

Before long, a pizza box added to his packages, they arrived at Francesca's rented ground-floor flat situated in a converted old house in a leafy side street near one of the town's large parks. It was a long way away from the part of town she had grown up in, he noted, understanding the relevance of her choice and wondering if it had been a conscious decision on her part.

Following her inside, he looked around with interest. It was not where he had imagined her staying, but the small, open-plan living space was clean and bright. There were a few personal touches…some colourful scatter cushions and throws on the old but comfortable armchairs and sofa, a few animal pictures on the walls, but no family photographs. Not that he had expected those. Any spare wall space was taken up with shelves filled with an abundance of books covering everything from biographies and environmental sciences to a wide range of fiction.

'This is a great place,' he commented, watching as she fetched plates and glasses of water from the galley-style kitchen.

Her nose wrinkled endearingly as she made a dissatisfied face. 'It'll do, for now. It was all I could afford when I first came back to town but at least I have a view of the hills and, being on the ground floor, I have access to the garden—tiny as it is.'

'You're planning on moving?'

'One day,' she confided, handing him a cutter for slicing the pizza.

Luke heard the wistful note in her voice. 'You still want your cottage in the woods?' he asked, as he divided up the food.

'You remember that?'

He looked up to see her watching him, her eyes widened in surprise. 'Sure. I remember everything about you, Chessie.'

The hint of a blush pinkened her freckle-dusted cheekbones, but it was the sudden wariness in her expression that had him backing off and changing the subject. There would be time, he hoped, in the days and weeks ahead to tell her about the house, to take her to the home he had bought on impulse four years ago, the home for which he now had such high hopes.

They talked about work and the hospital as they ate. He learned about some of his soon-to-be colleagues, well aware that Francesca confined herself to general details, unsurprised that she refused to indulge in gossip. The closest she came was when he asked about Olivia Barr, the A and E nurse who had abandoned his mother eight weeks ago.

'Olivia has a reputation around the hospital,' she allowed with evident disapproval.

Fascinated and aroused by the way in which Francesca finished her final slice of pizza and then sensuously licked her fingers clean, it took him a moment to concentrate on the conversation. 'What kind of reputation?'

'As a man-chaser.' A hint of mischief twinkled in silver-grey eyes. 'I'm sure you'll be meeting her very soon.'

'I hope not. Nurse Barr will, too, when I tell her what I think of the way she neglected my mother,' he added, smiling at the gleam of satisfaction Francesca failed to mask.

Their meal finished, he helped her clear up, reluctantly declining her tentative offer of coffee. He wanted more than anything to stay, but he knew he had to leave early. Far better that she wanted more, was disappointed their time together was over for now, than he risk outstaying his welcome and rushing her.

'Ma sent this specially for you,' he told her, handing her the plain bag he had brought with him and left on the kitchen worktop. 'Some of her almond shortbread, freshly baked this afternoon.'

'Oh…'

To his horror, he saw the welling of tears in smoky grey eyes as she turned away from him. 'Chessie, what is it?' he demanded, cursing himself for unwittingly upsetting her.

'Nothing.' She shook her head, her back to him, but he saw her lift a hand to wipe across her cheeks. 'Sorry.'

Resting his hands on her shoulders, he gently turned her round, tipping her face up with a thumb under her chin. 'Ma thought you liked it.'

'I do. It's not that. I…'

Even white teeth worried the fullness of her lower lip igniting a storm of needy desire within him. He wanted to do that…to taste her, nip her, kiss her. Cupping her face, focusing on her turmoil and not his own, he looked into the now dark pools of her eyes.

'Talk to me. Tell me what's wrong,' he whispered persuasively, revelling in the feel of silky soft skin beneath his palms.

'It's silly.'

He lightly pressed the pad of one thumb to her lips to halt her protest. 'Not if it upset you. Why?'

'Your mum gave me some once. It was my birthday and it was the only gift I had. I ran away from her because her warmth and the genuineness behind the giving made it priceless to me and I didn't want her to see me cry,' she admitted, a catch in her voice. 'The shortbread smelled wonderful. And I remember it was still warm from the oven. I couldn't resist it. My mother found me tucking into the first piece and she was furious with me for deviating from her regimented dietary plan.' Luke's throat hurt as Francesca tried to laugh, her chin lifting in defiance even as she was unable to look at him. 'She snatched the bag away from me and crumbled all the rest of the shortbread into the dustbin. I was punished for days afterwards for eating any of it.'

Feeling the pain of the girl she had been, Luke pulled her close, wrapping his arms round her, needing the hug as much as she did. He felt furious rage at Francesca's mother, a woman who had kept her daughter on such a tight leash, determined, it seemed, to live her own failed athletic dreams through Francesca, and making the girl's life hell with strict rules and training and an obsessive regime, making her an outcast because of her difference. Something he knew all about from his own family circumstances and the reason he and Francesca had understood each other all those years ago.

She felt impossibly good resting against him as he stroked a hand up and down her back, the satin strands of her fiery hair, still restrained in its braid, brushing against his skin. He wanted to hold her for all eternity but as his body reacted instinctively to her closeness, he drew back before she became aware of his arousal.

Knowing she was embarrassed, he lightened the moment, opening the bag and feeding her a piece of shortbread. 'Go on, be a devil,' he teased, smiling as she laughed and took a big bite.

Crumbs clung to her lips and chin, her tongue-tip peeping out to try and catch them. His stomach in knots, Luke couldn't resist brushing her skin clean with his fingers, trying to ignore the flare of surprise and awareness in Francesca's eyes as he touched her.

'Good?' he asked, hearing the roughness in his own voice.

'Amazing.' She giggled endearingly as she talked with her mouth full, swallowing before she continued. 'They're even more delicious than I remembered. Please thank your mum for me.'

Luke wrapped up the rest of the almond short-bread and left it on the counter for her. 'You can thank her yourself—she'd love to see you.'

'OK,' she agreed after a moment, her smile shy.

'Right, I'd best go and leave you to get a good night's sleep.' Reluctantly, he walked back into the living area and picked up his leather jacket from the back of the sofa. 'Thanks for the company. I've really enjoyed this evening.'

'Me, too.'

At the front door, he hesitated. Somehow he resisted the urge to kiss her senseless, knowing he would never leave if he once tasted the sweetness of her mouth. Instead, he brushed his lips across her forehead and forced himself to move back.

'I'll see you at work tomorrow.' He enjoyed one last lingering look at her before turning away. 'Sweet dreams, Chessie.'

His steps carried him swiftly back to his mother's house where he collected his car and drove home—alone—hot and needy for Francesca. Tomorrow couldn't come soon enough. He thought of her, of all she had been through in the past with her controlling mother, and vowed to ensure that she always felt safe and secure and had everything she wanted to make her own decisions for her future.

He just hoped above all else that he could share that future with her.

CHAPTER FOUR

FRANCESCA knew the instant that Luke stepped up behind her. Her whole body tingled, her pulse raced and heat percolated through her, pooling low in her belly. He let out a low whistle as he leaned in closer to look at the images on the screen. So close she could scent his earthy, musky fragrance and feel the heat of his body transferring to hers.

'That is some break.' His warm breath whispered across the skin of her neck as he spoke, stirring the loose strands of hair that had escaped her braid.

'Nasty,' she managed to murmur in agreement, fixing her gaze on the X-rays, struggling to maintain her professionalism. 'What will you do?'

The motorcyclist had been knocked from his bike by a hit-and-run driver shortly after one on

Friday morning. He had been rushed the ten miles from one of the outlying villages to Strathlochan Hospital by ambulance, the paramedics rightly concerned about haemorrhaging inside the thigh. The A and E team had stabilised the patient and paged Orthopaedics and Radiology—which had brought Luke and herself to the department as they were both on call for the night shift.

Despite the doctors immobilising the leg in a splint and administering analgesics, the man was still in pain. Unsurprising, Francesca thought as she looked at the multiple breaks. His femur was fractured in two places high up the shaft, while the tibia was broken, with a sheared-off fragment, and the fibula had snapped, one end piercing the skin.

Luke brushed against her as he reached to change the images to view the fractures from another angle. 'We'll have to put a nail and screws in the femur and plates on the tib and fib.'

'Looks like you'll be in Theatre for a while.'

'Sure does. Good thing I always liked Mechano kits and fixing things.' Luke cast her a mischievous smile before turning back to linger a moment more, his expression serious as he studied the various digital X-rays she had

taken. 'I'll call Maurice. He'll want to come in
for this one. And with so much bleeding, as well
as all the dirt in the wound and the risk of infection with an open fracture, we won't delay operating.'

As he moved away to talk with Robert Mowbray,
the A and E consultant in charge of the patient,
Francesca breathed out a sigh of relief and endea-
voured to get her wayward responses back under
control. This had been going on for nearly ten days
now and, despite her regular assurances to herself
that things would settle down, her awareness of
Luke seemed to get stronger every day.

From the first moment of the first day working
together in the fracture clinic, Francesca had
been impressed by and in awe of Luke's skill. He
knew what he wanted and didn't suffer fools
gladly, but even in Theatre during a tense operation—where she had seen other surgeons lose
their rag and take their temper out on assorted
staff—Luke never lost his cool and always
treated people with respect. She had quickly
realised that Luke had cultivated a work persona,
just as she had, reminding her once again just
how much they had in common.

They had swiftly fallen into a pattern, with

Luke walking her home after work, spending time with her, catching up on their lives without touching on anything too personal or relating to the past, talking mostly about work and their various experiences during their training. On one of their two days off between the change from day shifts to night shifts, she had gone with him to visit his mother. Sadie, recovered from her broken arm, had made her so welcome it had brought tears to Francesca's eyes.

In all their time together, Luke had done nothing to suggest he saw her as anything other than a friend, leaving her on each occasion with a gentle kiss to her forehead. And that was what she wanted…friendship. So why did she feel disappointed? Why did she yearn for more? And why did the frisson of sexual chemistry increase every time she saw him?

Another question also nagged at her. What was with their shifts? She had no idea how or why it came to be, but their working hours always seemed to match. When she was on call to A and E, so was Luke. When she was asked to cover the fracture clinic, he was taking it. When she was on nights, so was Luke. When she was called to the operating theatre to take images to verify the placement of fixings after repairs to fractures, Luke was there. She didn't want to ask if he had done something to arrange it, because she didn't want to appear stupid or for him to get the wrong impression. Maybe it was just an innocent coincidence and nothing to do with Luke at all, but suspicion lingered.

Not that she minded working with him. He was not only a superb doctor, sharply intelligent and exceedingly thorough, spotting things she knew others would have missed, but his attitude to his patients was wonderful. He exuded professional authority mixed with casual charm, he was kind and unhurried, and he listened. He knew when to tease and lighten the atmosphere, when to reassure and ease anxiety, and when to be firm and straightforward.

'Maurice is on his way,' Luke announced, appearing beside her and making her jump.

The sound of an ambulance siren cut through the night, its blue lights flashing in the darkness outside as it turned into the approach to the hospital. As the A and E staff swung into action to greet the new arrival, Luke caught her fingers and drew her aside, squeezing them gently before letting go.

'I don't know how long I'll be in Theatre,' he told her, the expression in his green eyes intent as he looked at her. 'But hopefully I'll catch up with you before breakfast and walk you home.'

'OK.'

Francesca wanted to tell him not to worry, that they didn't have to be joined at the hip and do everything together, but a worrying part of her wanted, *needed*, to see him.

His fingertips briefly skimmed her cheek. 'You look tired. I think we can both use these days off. If I don't see you before your shift ends, get home and have a good sleep. I'll call you later and we can arrange to do something over the weekend.'

Before she had a chance to respond, he strode off across the department, heading for the lift that would take him up to the floor that housed the operating theatres. She felt bemused. Her skin still tingled from his feather-light touch, and despite knowing it wasn't sensible to become so comfortable with him, to see him all the time, she was looking forward to it. She knew she was on dangerous ground, that she should be strong and keep more distance between them. Why hadn't she told him she already had plans for Saturday? She vowed that she would the next time she spoke to him. She would. Definitely.

'Francesca, good, you're still here.' A and E registrar Will Brown hurried up to her, reclaiming her attention. 'We have a collapsed man, aged seventy-two. Suspected abdominal aortic aneurysm with possible rupture. We've fast-bleeped the vascular surgeon, but we need chest and abdominal X-rays and an ultrasound scan.'

'Of course,' Francesca agreed, hurrying with him to Resus.

It was nearly half past two in the morning and things didn't seem to be slowing down. Whilst she didn't want anyone hurt or sick, having her attention focused on work and those who needed her meant she had less time to think disturbing thoughts about Luke.

The haemorrhaging under control and a femoral nail having been inserted in the motorcyclist's thigh, held in place by screws, Luke prepared to work on the lower leg under the watchful eye of Maurice Goodwin. Other members of the team had already thoroughly cleaned the wounds of dirt and gravel and had debrided dead and contaminated tissue.

Things were fairly relaxed under Mr Goodwin's regime, with classical music playing in the background and a lot of banter flowing back and forth between the staff…the kind his previous boss and mentor, Professor James Fielding-Smythe, would have hated.

Luke tuned out the chatter, and the relentless march of time, as he concentrated on his work, making an incision and sliding a metal plate under the muscles and along the tibia. After manoeuvring the fragment of bone that had splintered off back into place, he positioned the plate and attached it with several screws, bringing the pieces into alignment and holding them together, checking all the time on the X-ray display screen that everything was in the right place.

Next Luke turned his attention to the fibula and the jagged break that had pierced the skin. Here he used a smaller plate for the thinner bone, inserting screws and squeezing the fracture together, watching the screen again to ensure the correct alignment. Then all that remained was to suture the incisions closed and temporarily cover the wounds with sterile dressings to help guard against infection.

'Good job, Luke,' Maurice Goodwin praised

when the operation finally ended and their patient was taken to Recovery before being moved to the intensive care unit. 'He'll have a long recovery ahead of him but he has a good chance of full use of the leg eventually after your repairs.'

'Thank you, sir. Sorry we had to bring you in.'

The older man waved a dismissive hand before stripping off his protective clothing. 'All part of the job. Interesting case. I'll get back home for a couple more hours' sleep. Call me if there are problems,' he instructed before heading out.

Luke went to get cleaned up and change his clothes before going to ICU to check on the motorcyclist. All being well, he'd see him settled before his shift finished. Two of his colleagues were in the washroom when he entered. He'd kept himself pretty much to himself during his first ten days, interacting well on a professional level but resisting any social connections.

'So, Luke, what have you got that we haven't?' one of the junior doctors teased.

Wary, Luke glanced up from scrubbing his hands at the sink. 'What do you mean?'

'You seem to be having more success than the rest of the male population around here in chipping away at the Ice Maiden's chilly armour.'

Luke's temper rose as the two men laughed. 'I beg your pardon?'

'Francesca Scott,' the second doctor enlightened him with a salacious grin, apparently not reading the signs of Luke's ire. 'Many have tried and been frozen in the process, mate. Rumour is perhaps she's only into women, you know? Be a waste, though, right? I mean, she has a lush pair of breasts! Enough to make a man weep. If you have any luck warming her up, let me know. I wouldn't be the only one who'd like a turn.'

His fists clenched instinctively and it was only with a supreme effort of will and an inbuilt reminder that he was not his father or his brothers, solving everything with violence, that kept Luke from landing a punch on both the younger men's cocky, leering faces. No way would these creeps be touching Francesca. Neither would anyone else. If he ever caught them so much as looking at her breasts, they might discover there was more of the Devlin in him than he wanted there to be.

'You know nothing about Francesca and I don't appreciate you disrespecting her. I wouldn't do it again,' he advised curtly, walking away to the locker room, aware the two juniors were staring after him in surprise.

Once alone, Luke drew in a steadying breath. The comments from his colleagues made him wonder why Francesca had cultivated her reputation for coldness and unapproachability when he knew neither was true. A frown darkened his brow as he thought back, wondering what had happened to her in the ten years he had missed out on and if there were clues there he had yet to discover. He knew she'd had a rough time with that domineering, driven woman for a mother. Francesca had been so oppressed, pushed relentlessly to do something he wasn't at all sure she had enjoyed. And she'd been kept on such a tight leash she had known no fun, no joy, had not been allowed friends or any freedom. He recalled what she had told him about the incident with his mother's shortbread and renewed hurt for her tightened his gut.

His father and his brothers might have been bastards who belonged in the gutter, but at least he'd had his ma, had known some love and affection. How much of that had ever been in Francesca's life? Luke ran a hand through his hair. What else had happened to her? Was it just because of her mother that she shied away from relationships, from caring? Or had something else happened in the last decade that had hardened her resolution to remain alone? He needed her, badly, and he believed more and more that she needed him, too…needed to learn to love and be loved.

He changed scrubs, wrote up his notes and went to the ICU to check on his patient, all duties he had to perform before he was free to go in search of Francesca. With every day that passed, he was filled with renewed determination to stay close to her, to win her round, to show her how good things could be between them. Now they had some time off and he had plans for the weekend….

'It's only a few more weeks until Gina's wedding and we're going for the final fitting of dresses on Saturday,' Holly Tait, a nurse from the children's ward, explained to the small group gathered at a table in the canteen.

Francesca allowed the talk to wash over her. She'd sat with Holly because she liked her. Around the same age as herself, Holly was a great nurse…she was also shy and didn't gossip. Unfortunately, several others had come to join them as night shifts drew to an end, and Francesca wished she had just gone home as she usually did rather than come up here for some breakfast first. She'd told herself it was because she was too tired to be bothered to eat anything when she got home, but she very much feared it was all down to weakness of will and a traitorous part of her was lingering in the hope of seeing Luke.

'Are you coming to Gina's hen party, Francesca?' Holly asked, reclaiming her attention.

'If I'm not working.'

It was a cagey answer, she knew. She didn't enjoy social occasions and hen nights were usually the worst of the worst. But she liked Gina, and knowing that her celebrations were different from the norm made her reconsider. Instead of some wild, boozy night, Gina had planned a day of being pampered at a spa for a select group of friends, followed by an evening meal at a favoured restaurant. That she had been included on the guest list made Francesca feel both honoured and nervous.

The talk moved on, the girls giggling as they discussed how lucky Gina was to have won the heart of her rich and sexy Italian doctor. Seb Adriani had fallen so in love with Gina he had left his home country to come to Strathlochan to work alongside her at the drop-in centre.

'Well, I'm pleased for her,' Holly said, ever

loyal in her support. 'Seb is a really nice guy and they are so in love.'

'She deserves her happiness,' Francesca agreed, knowing how Gina had devoted so much of herself to care for her elderly grandparents. Her grandmother was still alive and Seb had embraced the older lady, insisting she be part of their family after their marriage.

She shared a smile with Holly, seeing the sadness behind the other girl's eyes, knowing from Annie how much Holly was in love with A and E doctor Gus Buchanan. It was a difficult situation because Holly's devious, manipulative sister Julia had all but stolen Gus from under Holly's nose, getting pregnant and trapping him into an unhappy marriage.

'Do you remember your first kiss?'

The question from one of the other nurses startled Francesca from her reverie. 'Um, yes. Do you?'

'I'll say.' Carolyn giggled, leaning forward to share her confidence. 'It was foul! But most people say that, don't they?'

The others joined in and they all laughed over their stories and memories of their first kisses. 'How about you, Francesca?' Carolyn asked.

'Me?' A flush warmed her cheeks. She seldom found herself in this sort of situation and hated to talk about herself, but memories of that first kiss were so vibrant in her mind she found herself replying. 'It was…nice.'

Nice? Who was she kidding? It had been perfect, wonderful. And even though they had both been so young and she had been so inexperienced, nothing had really lived up to it since. Which was ridiculous, but true all the same.

'Well, go on, then!' the girls teased.

'What?'

'You seem to be the only one of us who enjoyed their first kiss! Mine was wet and sloppy and revolting and I vowed never to do it again.' Holly giggled shyly.

'Mine was gross, too, but I've made up for it since!' another joked. 'Come on, Francesca.'

'There's not much to tell,' she lied, silent for several moments as she relived that unforgettable day in her mind…

It had been exam time near the end of the school year. She had been sixteen, surrounded in the school playground by the gang of girls who had tormented and teased her for as long as

Francesca could remember. Luke had come outside and the girls had jostled her, pushing her forward, bumping her into Luke and daring her to kiss him. She had been mortified as they had stood back to giggle and make catcalls. Tears had stung her eyes as she had forced herself to look up at Luke—eighteen, so handsome, her hero. He had looked past her to the group of girls, had realised what was going on, and the expression in his green eyes had gentled.

'Are they making you do this?'

She'd nodded, too shy and humiliated to speak.

'Well, let's give them a show they won't forget.'

'What?' Her eyes had widened, round and scared. 'You don't have to.'

He'd smiled then, the sinful, bad-boy smile that still made her melt. 'I know. But I want to kiss you,' he had confided, shocking her anew.

'Y-you do?' she'd managed, scarcely able to breathe.

'Very much.'

'But...'

He'd looked down at her, considering. 'Have you been kissed before?'

A tide of embarrassed colour had washed her cheeks as she shook her head in denial.

'Do you trust me?'

'Yes.'

The affirmation was immediate. She had always trusted him, despite the things they had said about him and his beastly family. Instinctively, she had always known that Luke and his mother were good people, and for years Luke had been her silent protector, always in the background but there if she'd needed help. Her skin tingled unbearably as he raised a hand, his fingers gliding along her cheek before sliding back into the untamable fall of hair, drawing her towards him.

'Just relax and follow my lead,' he whispered. 'I'll look after you.'

Drawing in a ragged breath, she nodded, eyes drifting shut at the feel of his lips as they pressed gently and firmly against hers. He was wonderful. She could hear the taunts and whistles from the girls but all she could focus on was him. He pulled away slightly and she experienced a crushing sense of disappointment that it was over, but he didn't let her go. Eyes sultry with something she didn't recognise, he brushed the pad of his thumb over her lips.

'Open your mouth for me, Chessie,' he instructed softly, using the name only he called her.

'W-what?'

He smiled, amused but kind. 'I want to do this right.'

A bit bemused, she nevertheless did what he said, her lips parting as he tilted her head and his mouth took possession of hers once more. There was no other way to describe it. Gently, firmly but thoroughly, he possessed her, teaching her what kissing was like. The world ceased to exist beyond their own space as his lips caressed hers. Then she started in shock as his tongue teased her lips before sliding inside her mouth. Even more shocking, she found she liked it. More than liked it. And she kissed him back, tentatively touching her tongue to his, gasping as he kissed her more deeply, more strongly, drinking her in, tasting and savouring her as if unable to get enough.

'Devlin!' His name, bellowed across the yard, made them jerk apart.

Dazed, she stared up at Luke as his hands dropped away from her, his expression a mix of desire, sorrow, anger and resignation as the teacher came up and shoved him.

'Get your hands off her.' The order had been unnecessary as they had no longer been touching. 'The headmaster's office. Now.'

As Luke was marched off like a criminal, Francesca had followed behind, determined he would not be punished just because of who he was, because of his awful father and brothers. Her anger had flared at the unfairness. It wasn't right, she wouldn't let it happen. By the time she had caught up with them, ignoring the secretary and stepping into the office, Luke was already being lambasted.

'Excuse me,' she interrupted, unsure where her courage was coming from.

Three pairs of eyes watched her, one shocked and concerned, two hostile.

'There's no need for you to be involved here,' the head told her.

'But there is. Luke's done nothing wrong, sir. *I* kissed *him*. I walked up to him and asked if I could kiss him. He did nothing to me. He didn't hurt me, or do anything against my will. It's not fair to blame him or treat him like this.'

Silence followed her impassioned speech.

'Why would you do such a stupid thing?' the head growled at her. 'He's not the sort of person you should be associating with. What would your mother say? He's bad news.'

'I don't believe that, sir. Luke's not responsible for his family. You can't do this. You can't blame him when it wasn't his fault. If you want to punish someone, it should be me.'

Her gaze met Luke's then and she saw his shock, his admiration, then he shook his head, trying to tell her to back off, to leave him, but she wouldn't, she was too angry at the injustice of it….

The clatter of a tray being dropped on the canteen floor snapped Francesca back to the present.

She didn't know to this day what all the fuss had been about over the kiss, but she had been dismissed and all but frogmarched back to her classroom. She had no idea what had happened after that as she had only seen Luke a few times in the distance, but never alone. She had never been able to talk to him, to do more than exchange lingering eye contact. A couple of weeks later he had sat his final exam, and then he had gone and she had never seen him again—until ten days ago.

But she had never forgotten him or that kiss.

She'd been kissed since then but nothing had compared to that first time. Which she knew was silly as she'd had no idea what she'd been doing and Luke had been scarcely more than a boy at the time, however much more experienced than her. But a connection had flowed between them, one she couldn't explain.

'It was enjoyable,' she said now with classic understatement, censoring her story, the girls agog as they listened. 'He was kind,' she continued, refusing to give them his name. 'He made it good, special.'

'Wow!' Holly breathed.

'Yeah,' Carolyn agreed. 'I wish my first kiss had been like that.'

'We need a male opinion,' one of the other nurses declared. 'Here's our hunky new surgeon, we'll ask him.'

Francesca smothered a groan as she turned her head in time to see Luke enter the room. Still dressed in scrubs, he looked tired and rumbled. He hesitated as the nurse called his name and beckoned for him to join them, but then Francesca's breath hitched as his gaze met hers and he headed in their direction with deceptively lazy strides.

'Ladies,' he greeted them.

Holly smiled in welcome. 'Hi, Luke.'

'We were talking about first kisses and we want a man's opinion,' Carolyn explained.

'Oh?'

Francesca kept her head down, unable to meet his gaze, wondering if he remembered, sure that he didn't.

'What was your first kiss like, Luke?' the nurse who had called him over asked.

'I don't remember my first ever kiss, but I remember one in particular.'

Francesca's breath lodged in her throat at Luke's words. Glancing up from beneath her lashes, her gaze clashed with his intense green one.

'Tell us,' Carolyn encouraged, almost bouncing on her chair with excitement.

'I kissed a girl at school,' Luke admitted, his voice husky. 'It was good, special.'

He'd unwittingly echoed her own words, Francesca realised, her cheeks warming again. She hoped none of the girls had noticed and that they wouldn't make the connection between her account and his. With a last lingering look in her direction, Luke excused himself. His parting words, that he was getting a quick coffee to go before changing and heading home, seemed to hold a silent message for her alone.

She finished up her breakfast, nerves fluttering inside her as she said a casual goodbye to her companions and headed out of the canteen. She took the stairs down to the ground floor and went outside, unsurprised when Luke, dressed now in jeans, jumper and his leather jacket, caught her up several minutes later as she wheeled her bicycle across from the covered shed. The hospital car park was filling up quickly as staff arrived for their day shifts and patients came for appointments or to book into wards for scheduled procedures and longer stays.

They walked down the hill in silence. It wasn't uncomfortable but it *was* charged. Francesca felt tired after three hectic night shifts on duty, but inside she was buzzing. She couldn't stop thinking about that kiss ten years ago…or help wondering what it would be like to kiss Luke now. Did he really remember what had happened between them or had his words just been a coincidence, something neutral to say in response to a group of women's nosy questions?

'How did the surgery go?' she finally asked,

needing normalcy to get her back on an even keel.

'It went well.' Luke's voice, warmly husky, sent tingles through her, and she tried to concentrate as he continued. 'Provided the wounds heal well and he doesn't get an infection, he'll be up on crutches within a few days, but he won't be able to weight-bear on the leg for five or six weeks in case the plates warp. He could need some physiotherapy to strengthen his muscles, but in time he should make a good recovery.'

Francesca smiled, proud of his skill and achievement, knowing from the X-rays she had taken in A and E that repairing the fractures would have been challenging. 'That's great.'

'Let's hope the hit-and-run driver who left him like that is caught.'

'Indeed.' She wasn't sure how likely it was, though. 'Were there any witnesses?'

Luke shrugged, but the casualness of the gesture belied his concerned expression. 'I don't know. I hope we'll get feedback from the police soon.'

The conversation ended as they reached her front door. Francesca opened it and wheeled her bicycle inside the wide hallway before leaning it against the wall. Turning she discovered Luke had waited on the doorstep. She knew it was best that he didn't linger now—they both needed their sleep—but the sense of disappointment was still strong. Squaring her shoulders and mustering her resolve to keep more distance between them, she walked back to the door to say goodbye.

'Get some rest,' he advised before she could speak. 'I'll see you tomorrow, Chessie.'

'I—'

Her words of denial and her determination to tell him she had other plans were lost as Luke bent his head and brushed her mouth with his. She froze, her stomach tightening with the painful thrill of awareness and desire. As he drew back a scant centimetre, she saw mischief sparkling in his green eyes.

'Open your mouth, Chessie,' he whispered.

She gasped. 'You *do* remember!'

'Of course.' His eyes darkened. 'I've never forgotten. Have you?'

'No,' she breathed, unconsciously moistening dry lips with the tip of her tongue.

'Care to try it again?'

She stared at him, heat coursing through her

veins. 'We shouldn't. I…' Her half-hearted protest trailed off.

'Chessie?'

All common sense was lost at the uncertainty, the need in his voice. 'Yes.'

A small smile, a mix of relief and triumph, curved his mouth at her surrender. Then his lips were on hers once more, soft, teasing, tempting. Her own parted for him, her hands rising of their own accord so she could sink her fingers into the thick, surprisingly soft strands of hair at the back of his head, urging him to stop playing and to kiss her properly. And he did. Oh, how he did!

She had fantasised about this and now it was happening. A whimper escaped as she sank into him, losing herself in the kiss. It was all heat and fire and passion, stirring things that had never been stirred before, making her want as she had never wanted before. Her knees felt unable to support her as Luke sucked on her tongue, drawing her into the warm, moist cavern of his mouth, and she pressed herself closer, alarmed at the terrible ache squeezing inside her, desperate for him to alleviate it.

His touch, his taste, inflamed and excited her. She couldn't breathe but decided she didn't care.

Who needed oxygen? She was plugged into Luke's life force and everything she needed for survival came from him. He was familiar and yet enticingly different. Better. So much better the man than the boy. She gave herself up to the magic, drugged by the consuming, deeply erotic sensuality of the man, her whole body trembling as his arms tightened around her, his hands skimming down her back to cup her rear, drawing her against him, making her intensely aware of his arousal.

Kissing him back, matching him move for move, her tongue twining with his, she gave everything and he took it, the flare of passion between them so strong and unexpected and remarkable that she could think of nothing else, of no one else but Luke and how wonderful he made her feel. She wanted him to lay her down there and then on the hall floor and take all of her.

It was the shock of that very realisation that brought her senses struggling back. They broke apart, gasping air into parched lungs, and she saw that the hot passion in Luke's green eyes matched what she was feeling.

'Dear God,' she whispered hoarsely.

'Yeah.'

She forced her hands to loosen their hold on him and stepped back, frightened by what had happened and all she had felt, part of her wanting it, part of her fighting just as hard against it.

'Luke—'

Two fingertips pressed against swollen, well-kissed lips, silencing her. 'Don't say anything. Don't close your mind to this, Chessie, please. Give it time—give *us* time.'

His plea brought a lump to her throat, her whole body quivering as he whispered the pad of his thumb across her cheek in a heart-stopping caress. Green eyes shone with sincerity, vulnerability and the kind of sinful sensuality that always undid her. She couldn't form a single word to deny him.

Taking advantage of her momentary docility, Luke brushed his lips across her forehead, released her and moved back. 'Sleep well, Chessie. We'll talk later,' he decreed.

And then he was gone. It was several moments before Francesca could gather her scattered wits, then she closed the front door, locked it and sagged back against the solidness of the wood, every atom of her being zinging in reaction and craving more of Luke. Much more.

Once again she had failed to stick to her plan. She had not sent Luke away. Legs shaking and feeling as if they no longer belonged to her, she made her way to her bedroom, drawing her curtains against the low April sunshine before stripping off her clothes and crawling under the duvet.

She was bone weary and yet she felt too wired to sleep. And she knew, when sleep did come, it would be filled with dreams of Luke…of his touch, of his taste, of his musky masculine scent, and of the sincerity of his words.

What was she going to do?

CHAPTER FIVE

'IF YOU want to help yourself to some coffee, I'll just take a quick shower and get changed.'

As Francesca disappeared, Luke let out a shaky breath and, following her invitation, headed to the kitchen. He hadn't handled things well in the last twenty-four hours and he was well aware he had ground to make up if he wasn't to unnerve Francesca even further. Having been unable to sleep all day on Friday after their steaming kiss had left him hot and hard, he had phoned her in the evening, desperately needing to hear the sound of her voice.

She had been edgy, confirming what he had already acknowledged to himself—that he had succumbed to the temptation to kiss her far too soon. But all that stuff in the hospital canteen about first kisses had brought *their* first kiss vividly to mind, and he hadn't been able to resist finding out what it was like to kiss her ten years on, the woman rather than the girl. Magical, he had discovered. But just as it had the first time, things had spun out of control at the first taste of her and it had turned into something much more than a simple kiss. Now Francesca was trying to distance herself.

When he had asked about today, Saturday, she'd told him she already had plans. He wasn't sure how genuine that was but it had made him think. He'd realised how arrogant he had been to assume Francesca would spend her time with him, but he had needed to see her straight away, to steady things between them before she had too much time to think, to talk herself out of getting close to him and back away.

So he had been hugely relieved to finally persuade her to have breakfast with him after her morning jog. That she was running at all, given her background, interested him, and he wanted to know more about that. What he hadn't expected was to arrive early and walk to the park to meet her, only to find her jogging with another man. That had nearly doubled him over with shock and alarm.

Pottering around her kitchen, he tried to

block out the sound of the shower, his imagination far too fertile as he pictured her stripping off her baggy tracksuit and stepping under the spray, water sluicing over her silky soft, freckle-dusted ivory skin. His body reacted in a predictable way and it was pure effort of will that prevented him storming down the corridor and joining her in the hot, steamy cubicle.

'Damn.'

Cursing himself, he focused ruthlessly on his task, setting out the treats he had brought from the nearby bakery for breakfast...still-warm, soft granary rolls, local honey and a couple of fruity Danish pastries. He poured glasses of juice and helped himself to a cup of the coffee Francesca had left brewing when she had left the house. Which brought him back to her jogging and seeing her with another man.

Since he had been introduced to her running companion, Frazer McInnes, a flight doctor on Strathlochan's air ambulance—and his six-months-pregnant wife, Callie—his heart was slowly settling back into its normal rhythm again. The event had shown him not only how little he still knew about Francesca's life now, and her friends, but how complacent he had become. He had a lot of work to do yet before he could ever relax and feel he had won her over to give a relationship between them a fair chance.

Now they needed to talk about deeper issues, the topics they had been avoiding for the last ten days…the past, his father, her mother. He hoped to persuade Francesca to spend the day with him tomorrow and accompany him on an errand he'd been asked to run for the prof—visiting another of his former protégées now living in a village some miles west along the Solway coast. The journey would give them captive time to talk about difficult things. And spending a bit of time with husband-and-wife doctors Conor and Kate Anderson would allow Francesca to see that a healthy, functioning, equal relationship was not only possible, it was normal. Quite different from the homes either Francesca or he himself had grown up in.

As for today, it had started with a setback but he had not lost all hope of them spending the day together. The shower stopped and a few moments later he heard a door close. He had a only few moments left to compose himself and prepare to break through the new defences Francesca was trying to place between them. Stage one was to find out what she was doing today and to wangle an invitation to join her. Stage two was to win her acceptance to go with him tomorrow.

And top of his mental list was the instruction to exercise some self-control. Whatever the temptation, he was *not* to kiss her again anytime soon, at least not until he had regained lost ground. Quite how difficult it would be to keep all his good intentions was obvious the moment Francesca joined him in the kitchen.

She was wearing walking boots, the soft, leg-hugging jeans with the rip in the thigh that had already given him sleepless nights, and a purple fleece top that enhanced the grey of her eyes and should have clashed with the vibrancy of her red hair, but didn't. Her face was bare of make-up, her ivory skin tinged with a dewy glow from the warmth of her shower, and her riot of long cork-screw curls was tied back in a loose ponytail, a few damp tendrils clinging to her neck. She looked natural, sexy and good enough to eat. And he was *very* hungry. Swallowing the lump that had formed in his throat, feeling the kick of his heart against his ribs, he hastily sat down at the table to hide his instant reaction to the sight of her.

As Francesca cast him a wary glance and took the seat across from him, Luke briefly closed his eyes and prayed for strength and deliverance.

How did she end up in these situations?

From beneath her lashes Francesca watched as Luke opened the gate and allowed her to precede him onto the path. She was strong, independent and used to being alone, so why had all her will-power and common sense deserted her? Despite the stern lecture she had given herself in the shower and all the good intentions she had mustered as she had walked into the kitchen, she had caved like a weakling under Luke's subtle persuasion during breakfast.

And here she was, spending the day with him in spite of her determination to the contrary. Not that she could fault his attitude when she had explained how she spent some of her time off volunteering at a local animal rescue centre. He'd been keen to come along, cheerfully throwing himself into the tasks he had been set, exercising dogs in the field and showing no sign of complaint or that he found the dirty job of cleaning out rows of dog and cat kennels distasteful or beneath him.

Now, after a snack lunch with the centre staff, came the best part of the day as far as Francesca was concerned—taking her two favourite dogs out for a long ramble. Sometimes she walked in the extensive grounds of Strathlochan Castle. The private gardens were closed to all but paying visitors on certain days of the year, but the current laird had opened up the rest of the estate for locals. Francesca enjoyed the rolling fields and the native woodlands. At other times she went further afield, up into the hills for longer, wilder, more solitary walks.

Today, with Luke, she chose the castle. The estate bordered one side of the loch that gave the town its name. The castle building itself was impressive, as was the magnificent scenery in which it was set with the backdrop of the hills. They passed the grand building and, beside it, the small chapel where Frazer and Callie had married on Christmas Eve.

The azaleas and rhododendrons, whose fat buds were almost ready to open, would make a spectacular show any day now but for the moment the last daffodils lined the more manicured pathways near the buildings. As they walked deeper into the countryside, the cultivated plants gave way to wildflowers, including celandines and wood anenomes. In another month or so the woods would be awash with bluebells. Pale blue skies held wispy streamers of white cloud, and she saw the first swallows skimming across the fields and around the farm buildings. They were early. Was that a sign of a good summer to come?

'How long have you been working at the rescue centre?' Luke asked as they headed deeper into the woods, the two dogs, Murphy and Harry, enjoying the freedom of being off the lead.

'Ever since I came back to Strathlochan. I was never allowed to have pets when I was a child,' she admitted, recalling her youthful disappointment and her craving for a friend, even a four-legged one.

Luke nodded, understanding in his eyes. 'Neither was I. I always wanted a dog.'

'Me, too. I'd take these two home today, but it's against my rental agreement to keep animals at the flat.' She sighed, watching what looked like two huge black teddy bears, hairy and cuddly, frolicking through the undergrowth, feathery tails wagging rhythmically. 'Besides, there's not enough space there for two hulking great Newfoundlands. It's such a shame, they've been at the centre for months and haven't found a home. Their former owners moved abroad for work and no one seems to want to take on two such big dogs at once. And such young, bouncy ones. They're only two years old. As brothers they've been inseparable, and they need to stay together, if possible.'

'One day…' Luke murmured, taking her hand and giving it a gentle squeeze.

'Yes.'

Lacking the motivation to pull away, she allowed Luke to link their fingers as they walked on along the path. Thoughts nagged at her. Why, when she was so bad with people, so awkward around them, did she always find Luke so easy to talk to? Being close to him generated discomfort but of a very different kind—because he made her burn with need and desire. And it took tremendous effort not to dwell on the spine-tingling, amazing kiss they had shared the previous morning. She was so aware of him, so attracted to him. It was as if all the cells and molecules in her body were somehow programmed and magnetised to be drawn to his. Two halves of one whole. But why? How could that be?

'I was interested to hear that you were still running,' Luke commented after a while, holding back a low tree branch so she could pass by without catching herself.

'I jog to keep fit now, nothing else.' She glanced at him, surprised that he had brought the subject up. 'Why?'

'Ma and I looked out for mentions of you in the local paper and watched when the junior trials and any other races were on television. But I always wondered why you did it. The running, the intensive training. If your mother pushed you as much I thought or if being a top athlete was what *you* really wanted.'

Amazed by his astuteness, she dragged her gaze from the disturbing intensity of his, halting as they emerged from the wood and turning to look at the view of the castle, loch and town spread out below them. Murphy and Harry, panting from their enthusiastic exertions, flopped to the ground in a patch of shade nearby, doggy grins on their faces.

'Chessie?'

'I did enjoy athletics—at first. When I was young and it was a hobby, it was fun,' she allowed after a long pause. 'You're right, it was my mother's dream, not mine, that I should become a success. She had delusions of grandeur and started thinking Olympic medals and the kind of substantial sponsorship deals that would give her a luxurious retirement.' Francesca paused, hearing the bitterness lacing her tone but unable to help it. When Luke's fingers tightened on hers, conveying his support, she continued. 'Once things became an obsession with her, it ruined any enjoyment for me. She started her rigid schedule, the strict diet, her rules for me and my behaviour—no friends, no distractions, no outside interests, just running and school. School came a poor second in her eyes and she'd take me out for days to travel to athletic meets around the UK.'

'How did you cope with all that pressure?' he asked, a frown on his face.

The breeze blew some escaped tendrils of hair across her face and she absently tucked them behind her ear with her free hand. 'I don't know. I hated standing out as so different from everyone else. Being shy didn't help. Despite

my mother's ambivalence about education, I recognised the importance of it for my future, and
hid myself away with my books whenever I
could.'

'Yeah, that sounds just like me.' Luke's smile
had a hard edge and it was her turn to express her
understanding of how difficult his upbringing
had been, squeezing his fingers as he had hers.
'My father demanded I leave school at sixteen
but I battled to stay on, knowing that my brain
was my only way out. I had no intention of
ending up like my father and brothers.'

'Your mum told me your father died a few
years ago. What happened to Jon and Pete?' she
asked now, giving in to her curiosity.

'Jon followed in our father's footsteps—last
we heard he was in prison for armed robbery.
Pete woke up to the mistakes he was making.
After my father died in jail, Pete cut out, moving
to America to make a new life for himself.
Neither of them keep in touch with Ma or me.'

Francesca turned more to face him, trying to
pick up the nuances in his changing expressions.
'That must be hard on her. Your mum is an
amazing lady, doing her best for all of you in
horribly difficult circumstances. I always

admired her. She didn't deserve all the hassle the others gave her, but how proud she must be of you.'

'Thanks, Chessie.' His soft words were accompanied by the gentlest of caresses as he brushed the back of his knuckles across her cheek. Her skin tingled with sensation. 'That means a lot to me. And despite all the bad stuff, I always knew I was blessed to have her. I wish you'd had that, too.'

Embarrassed, she shifted and turned back to stare at the view. Somehow, despite the difference in their backgrounds and upbringing, and the material privileges she'd had access to that had been denied to him, Luke had always seemed to understand that her life was less than perfect.

As the dogs stirred, gaining a second wind, they all started walking again, more slowly this time, taking the track that climbed slightly over open ground towards another stand of woodland. They paused by a stream that wound down the hillside, water-loving Murphy and Harry taking the chance for a drink and a paddle.

'How did you manage to break away from your mother's hold in the end?'

Luke's question sucked her back into the past. 'She became ever more zealous as time went by, as did my resentment.'

What she didn't voice was how protected she had felt with Luke around, how he had sheltered her from the worst of the bullying and name-calling. Until he had left. Then things had worsened for a while. But she couldn't tell him how miserable she had been for the two years after he had gone, her dislike and fear of her coach, her life governed by her mother's tight control and ever more unreasonable rules.

'Once I turned eighteen, Mother no longer had any legal control over me,' she continued. 'Things came to a head, we rowed horribly, and I found the nerve to pack up and leave it all behind, calling her bluff.'

'I've been there, I know how hard it is to make the break. You were brave to take the chance, Chessie,' Luke praised her, admiration evident in his voice. He raised their joined hands and pressed a kiss to the inside of her wrist, stealing her breath.

'I hitched to Edinburgh,' she told him when she could speak again. 'I made ends meet by working two part-time jobs, one in a bookshop and one in a supermarket, while I waited for my exam results and to begin my training as a radiographer.'

She thought back to those difficult days, the awful shared flats she had endured, doubly hard because she had found it so scary to be in close proximity to strangers. Having succeeded professionally, she was slowly building a nest egg. She carefully managed her budget, renting her small but adequate flat when she returned to Strathlochan, riding a bike rather than running a car, searching charity shops for clothing bargains. Anything to help her one day achieve the dream of security and buying her own home, preferably in a quiet rural spot outside town. She had the image of a house in mind, one she had coveted when she had been young. Although she knew she would never own it, it gave her a goal to strive for.

'And the running?'

'I put on a lot of weight when I first left home—an act of rebellion after my mother's control of my diet, weighing me every day, supervising everything I ate. So I indulged in all the foods I'd never been allowed, like chocolate and pizza,' she confessed, catching Luke's smile.

'You look wonderful.' His appreciative, leisurely appraisal from her head to her toes and back again made her flustered and brought a blush to her cheeks.

'I learned to find a balance, to enjoy eating what I wanted to combined with exercise. I started jogging...running on my own terms. But I knew deep inside that I would never let anyone else have control over me again.'

The import of Francesca's final words was not lost on Luke. After her years with her mother, it would always be important to her to make her own decisions and not feel closed in or trapped. It made his task even harder. As for her worries about her body, he could reassure her she was perfect. True, she had more flesh on her bones now than when she had been a young teenager, super-fit but bordering on too skinny. The new look was much more healthy...and sexier. All those lush and natural feminine curves fired his blood with desire.

'Where's your mother now?' he asked, trying to take his mind off his physical reaction to her.

'After the row she threw me out, realising I was no longer going to be her meal ticket. She sold the house and took off to Spain with her latest toy boy—he's something in computers and filthy rich. I've no idea if she's still there. I never see or hear from her.'

'I'm sorry.'

She shrugged. 'It doesn't matter.'

But he knew it did, knew how the pain and resentment never really went away. 'Why Edinburgh?' he asked, hoping to steer them onto safer ground.

'For years my mother told me that my father had left when I was born because he hadn't wanted me. I felt rejected, unloved, to blame.'

'Chessie—'

'It's true and she fostered those feelings, making me feel guilty and as if I owed her something,' she insisted, cutting off his attempt to refute her statement and tell her she had not been at fault. 'It was only when I turned eighteen and was searching for something in the loft that I found the letters that proved all my mother had told me was a pack of lies.'

Her words brought a sense of foreboding. 'What letters?'

'From my birth father, begging to see me. There were birthday and Christmas cards, presents, notes to me—all things I had known nothing about.'

'Why did she keep them?'

Francesca shook her head. 'I have no idea. The sense of power, maybe? That was what the final row was about. And why I went to Edinburgh eight years ago—to find him. But by then it was too late. The father who *had* loved me and who had been denied access to me had died several years previously. Likewise, I discovered too late the paternal grandparents I had never known existed. They were also gone. There was no one.'

Luke drew her closer, wanting nothing more than to hold her and take away her pain, his heart aching for her. In his mind they were two damaged people who needed each other. It was why he had come home to Strathlochan. Home to take care of his mother. But most of all home to Francesca—to claim her and to make sure she was never hurt or alone again. He had not counted on her mental and emotional toughness and her inner scars. Just how deeply and irrevocably her bitch of a mother had affected her was only now hitting home in its shattering entirety.

'What about your coach? What was his name?'

Instantly Francesca tensed beside him and he felt a tremor run through her. 'Alan,' she murmured, shivering as she spoke.

Luke halted their progress along the path, turning to face her, his eyes narrowing as he noted the pallor of her skin. Refusing to meet his gaze, she withdrew her hand from his, her fingers plucking nervously at the hem of her top. Dread pooling in the pit of his stomach, he reached out and cupped her chin, forcing her to look at him, suspicion darkening his mood and firing his temper.

'Did he touch you?'

'Luke…'

'Answer me, Francesca.' But he could see the truth in her eyes and it ate him up inside.

'My mother wanted to get into Alan's pants, he wanted to get into mine. She got hers, he didn't…not entirely.'

'And your mother did nothing to protect you?' he demanded.

'She told me to make nice to him because of what he could do for my career as a middle- and long-distance runner.' She sucked in a steadying breath, closing her eyes, and he waited for the rest of it, trying to tame his anger, not wanting to alarm her. 'Alan used to make me change in front of him. He watched me, touched me a time or two, but no more.'

Fury raged through Luke's gut. He wanted to track the bastard down and show him what he thought of him. 'Why didn't you tell me? I would have dealt with him.'

Grey eyes, bruised with confusion and hurt, looked up at him. 'It was after you had gone,' she finally whispered, and he swore viciously under his breath.

'God, Chessie, I'm sorry,' he rasped, drawing her into his arms, closing his eyes as he felt her body shaking.

'It wasn't your fault.'

Even as she sought to absolve him, he detected the lingering betrayal and pain his sudden disappearance had so clearly caused her. Yes, he had worried about her, but predominant at the time had been escaping his own hell. He'd not fully considered what his leaving might mean to Francesca, who'd had no one else around to watch over her. Little wonder she distrusted people, men especially, when so few of them had ever done anything right by her. No way would he ever let her down again.

He drew back, cupping her face in his hands, looking deep into her eyes. 'I remember the first time I saw you, coltish and pretty and with this amazing hair,' he told her with a smile, the fingers of one hand stroking the fiery mass of curls. 'I was drawn to you because I recognised your sadness and aloneness—they mirrored my own. We didn't speak much but I always felt close to you, understood you, wanted to protect you. I never forgot the day we kissed. Not only for the kiss itself, as unforgettable as that was, but because of the way you marched into the head's office afterwards and spoke up for me. God, you had guts, Chessie. Despite your shyness, you did that. For *me*. No one but Ma had ever fought my corner with me before. You humbled me, amazed me, made me feel I was more than I was, more than everyone else thought a Devlin could be.'

He came from the wrong side of the tracks, was a loner, had struggled all his life to escape his family's reputation. He had been labelled bad because of his father and his brothers. He'd never done anything wrong, but he'd been picked on and taunted all his life because of his surname. Aside from his mother, Francesca had been the only one who had been kind to him, who had understood him, believed in him. She had never judged him, but had stood up for him no matter the cost to herself.

No, he had never forgotten her, or their first kiss. She'd been sweet and pure and unimaginably exciting. He hadn't meant things to get so out of hand but he'd been mad at the way she was always picked on and, yes, damn it, he *had* longed to kiss her. He just hadn't anticipated it would be quite so thorough and consuming and arousing. Until they'd been caught and he'd been cast as the evil wrong-doer.

The dogs bounded around them, snapping him from his thoughts and back to the present. It was time to head back but not before he had explained something to Francesca.

'After the kiss, I was ordered to stay away from you at school. Outside it I could never get close to you because of your mother. The day I finished my final exam I got home to find my father starting on my mother. I hit back. It felt good to do it, to protect Ma, to not let him get away scot-free, but it meant I had to leave there and then or goodness knows what would have happened—to her or to me. I was hurt and bleeding. I grabbed my stuff, made my promise to Ma and headed south to London. I hated leaving her. And you. But I had no choice that day, Chessie. I feared what he would have done had I stayed.'

'Luke…'

Overwhelmed by powerful emotions, Francesca didn't know what to say, but she recognised the truth of his words. Inside she cried for what he had been through. The woman she was now was proud of him for all he had achieved. The girl she had been still felt hurt and confused and abandoned.

'As soon as I had established myself in London, I sent for Ma,' he told her, taking her hand again as they headed into the woods, taking the path that wound back down the hill towards the castle. 'She lived with me until my father died. With the threat from him gone, and with Jon and Pete having left town to follow their own paths to self-destruction or redemption, Ma was determined to move back to Strathlochan. I helped her buy the town house, and I bought a place for myself in case circumstances changed and I ever came back. It was a good investment, and it was rented out until recently. Now I've moved in.'

Luke's explanation surprised her—not that he had helped his mother but that he had owned a house here all that time. 'I had no idea.'

'I know.' He halted at the gate, turning to face her. 'Until two weeks ago I'd only come back to Strathlochan twice before in ten years. The first time I was twenty-one and I hadn't been able to forget you or stop worrying about you. I needed to see you, Chessie, to know you were all right, but Ma and I discovered you had left the previous year and no one knew where you or your mother had gone. I couldn't find you.'

He'd thought of her? Come back for her? Tried to find her? Francesca found it difficult to breathe as she considered the implications of Luke's admission. Before she could form any thoughts, let alone words, Luke opened the gate and they walked back down through the castle grounds towards the main entrance. As they neared the road, Luke let go of her hand so that they could call the dogs to them and put them back on their leads. She was uncomfortable to realise just how much she missed his touch and the contact between them. Murphy and Harry bounded up to them and she watched Luke make a fuss of them, warmed by the way in which he had befriended both the dogs. It meant a lot to her. Quite why it should matter increased her unease and confusion.

They made their way back to the rescue centre on the outskirts of town in silence. Francesca found her thoughts centred on Luke, not only on the meaning of all he had admitted to her but on the undeniable bond between them. She was drawn to him in a way she couldn't explain. He had always been a loner, just like her. In his teens he'd had a touch-me-not shield in which he had secmed to cloak himself, letting few people in. Except his mother. And, Francesca now realised with a sense of awe and uncertainty, herself. The past, the effects his father had had on him, still remained, scarring him, shaping him, but he'd broken free, had made something of himself, as she had instinctively known he would.

Talking to Luke made her aware of how much the years of her mother's control still affected her. True, she had made her own escape, but she had stepped out into the world alone…angry, scared, betrayed, and determined never to allow anyone else to gain control of her or her life again. Maybe that explained why she held something back from the friendships she had made since she had been back in Strathlochan. She was closest to Annie, but she had never told her anything about her past, her mother, her athletics, or allowed Annie to see the real person inside her. Only with Luke did she feel safe enough to be herself. That was both comforting and frightening.

Back at the rescue centre, she gave Murphy and Harry a hug, hating to see such social, people-loving dogs shut away in their run. She finished up her chores and then went to meet Luke, surprised to find him talking to the centre manager by the office. With a shock of white hair, Sally Hislop, now in her sixties, had devoted her life to animals. She had extraordinary energy and drive, and she was very much a maverick who didn't suffer fools gladly. Luke, it seemed, had passed Sally's test of acceptance.

'He's all right, this one,' Sally remarked as Francesca joined them. 'You can bring him back any time.'

High praise from Sally, Francesca knew. 'If he wants to,' she murmured, embarrassed and unsure how to respond.

'I definitely want to,' Luke admitted, sharing

what looked like a conspiratorial smile with Sally.

Puzzled, Francesca said her goodbyes and led the way outside, glancing up at the darkening clouds moving in over the distant hills. 'It looks like rain.'

'Sure does,' Luke agreed, unlocking the doors to his four-by-four. 'Hop in.'

Having promised herself she would spend some time away from Luke, she felt contrarily let down when the short drive to her flat was completed and he showed no sign of getting out of the car.

'Thanks for today,' she said, masking her unwanted disappointment as she unfastened her seat belt and opened the door.

'Thank *you*, Chessie. I had a lovely time.' Luke's hand on her arm prevented her leaving. 'Have you thought any more about tomorrow?'

She had, despite trying not to. She'd been shocked over breakfast when Luke had asked her to go with him to Glentown-on-Firth, a village to the west of Strathlochan. He had to deliver something on behalf of his former boss, Professor James Fielding-Smythe, he'd said, and had been asked to lunch with local GPs Conor and Kate

Anderson. She'd never met the Andersons, having avoided the twice-yearly, fundraising get-togethers arranged for all the region's health, fire, police and rescue services, but their names were familiar from request forms referring patients for X-rays, scans and other investigations.

'Um…' she hedged, undecided. Not only did the thought of meeting strangers daunt her, but she knew she should say no and keep some distance between Luke and herself. The trouble was, a traitorous part of her yearned to be with him. 'I don't know.'

'Please, Chessie. I'd really like you to come and keep me company. It would mean a lot to me.'

Oh, hell! How could she resist him when he used that low husky voice and turned that seductive, sultry green gaze on her? 'OK.' Her whispered agreement was out before she could halt it.

'Great!' Luke's smile sucked all the air from her lungs and turned her insides to mush. 'You're a star.'

He leaned across and pressed a chaste, all-too-brief kiss on her lips before moving away. Bemused, she slipped out of the car, finding her legs decidedly shaky.

'I'll pick you up at eleven in the morning,' Luke promised, restarting the engine. 'Bye, Chessie.'

'Bye.'

She closed the car door and headed up the path, turning to wave when she realised Luke was waiting to see her safely inside. He waved back. Even across the distance separating them she felt the potent touch of his gaze. Then he was pulling away from the kerb and she stepped inside and closed the door behind her.

The flat felt empty and unwelcoming as she walked restlessly around, changing her clothes and heading to the kitchen to make herself a cup of tea. There were still traces of Luke—the empty bakery bag left on the kitchen counter, the remains of the delicious local honey, the mug he had used for his coffee, washed and upturned on the drainer to dry.

A shiver rippled through her and Francesca wrapped her arms around herself. She wasn't cold. She was scared... scared that Luke was becoming far too important a fixture in her life.

Now she had agreed to spend the day with him tomorrow.

What was she doing?

And where was it all going to end?

CHAPTER SIX

FRANCESCA was no closer to answering any of her questions the next day. She sat beside Luke as he drove west towards Glentown-on-Firth, unable to make sense of her own warring feelings.

Telling herself that she wanted nothing more from Luke than friendship hadn't stopped her feeling horribly disappointed that he hadn't kissed her again. No more than a brief brush of his lips across hers as he had greeted her on arrival before he had introduced her to their unexpected travelling companion—an enormous cuddly elephant, who took up much of the backseat. The soft toy was the reason for their trip, she discovered, being Professor James Fielding-Smythe's present for Conor and Kate Anderson's daughter, Rebecca, whose third birthday was in a few days' time.

'Why an elephant?' she had asked, unable to help smiling.

'Apparently Conor and Kate were given sponsorship of an orphaned baby elephant in Kenya as a wedding present. They visited the elephant orphanage on their honeymoon and have continued to foster ever since,' Luke had explained, surprising her with the story. 'I gather Rebecca has always been fascinated with "their" baby, and elephants in general, and the prof knew she would love this toy.'

'It'll be bigger than she is!'

Luke's chuckle had filled her with warmth and a secret longing she had tried hard to ignore. 'More than likely.'

Overnight rain had left things fresh but after a cool start the April day was turning warm and sunny. As they left Strathlochan behind, Francesca sat back and enjoyed the countryside, acknowledging that Luke had been right…it was good to get out and have a change of scenery. She glanced back at the fluffy elephant and smiled again. The toy was going to swamp a three-year-old. Luke, ever thoughtful, had bought a card and a couple of storybooks for Rebecca's birthday and had invited Francesca to sign the card. It had felt strangely intimate to put her name next to his. He had also picked up a bottle of wine and some flowers for Conor and Kate.

They talked of neutral topics for most of the journey but Francesca found herself becoming more tense the closer they came to their destination. She knew little about the Andersons, so she asked Luke to fill her in before they arrived.

'I've only met them once myself.' His admission surprised her. 'They were in London for some reason a year or two ago, and stopped by the hospital to see the prof,' he continued. 'Kate Fisher, as she was when once a trainee on his team, left to follow her first love—general practice. He was very disappointed that she gave up surgery and, much to Kate's embarrassment, she was introduced to those of us working for him as the ideal we could never hope to emulate!'

'So how did she end up here—and still in touch with the professor?'

Luke glanced across and smiled. 'Now, there's a tale.'

'Go on,' she invited, intrigued.

'Kate volunteered for aid work in Africa. On her last stint she was caught up in some kind of civil war. Her brother was a freelance photojournalist working over there, too. I don't know all the details,' Luke admitted, his tone reflecting the seriousness of the situation, 'but Kate was alone and having to deal with unimaginable casualties. Her brother was killed. And then Kate was hurt herself but kept working. By the time she was found and evacuated, she was in bad shape.'

Shocked, Francesca was silent for a moment, wondering how on earth Kate had coped in such dreadful and frightening circumstances. 'What happened then?'

'I think Kate went through a crisis of confidence, unsure if she could still be a doctor.' Luke paused at a crossroads, checking the directions before making the turn down a quiet country lane. 'The prof has an old friend in Glentown-on-Firth and he comes up here once a year to see Fred. The pair of them go salmon fishing,' he continued with affectionate amusement. 'Anyway, he arranged with Fred for Kate to come here and do some locum work to ease her back in and give her a quiet environment in which to recover.'

'And it worked, obviously.'

'Absolutely.' Again Luke chuckled. 'Conor

was—is—Fred's partner in the practice. He and Kate fell in love. It took time, but Conor helped Kate conquer her demons and regain her confidence. They married not long afterwards and Kate settled here as another partner, allowing Fred to reduce his hours.'

It was a heart-warming story and Francesca couldn't help but be moved by it. Whilst she was interested in meeting the couple, she felt intimidated, too. She really wasn't good with people on a social level. She glanced down at what she was wearing, still uncertain about her outfit. It wasn't often that she wore dresses or skirts, but she had wanted to make an effort for the Andersons—and for Luke. From her eclectic wardrobe she had chosen a floaty patterned skirt in a mix of greens and blues, teaming it with a long-sleeved white top and flat shoes because of her height. She had tied her hair back in a loose ponytail, her wayward bouncy curls fanning down her back to her waist. From the appreciation in Luke's eyes when he had seen her—the memory of which still made her tingle—she looked OK.

Without the shield of her work persona, however, Francesca felt nervous. 'Conor and

Kate won't mind me coming with you, will they?' she fretted, her fingers fiddling with the catch of her bag which rested in her lap.

'Of course not. Don't worry, Chessie. They're looking forward to meeting you.'

Luke's comments did nothing to calm the flight of butterflies conducting aerobatic manoeuvres in her stomach. He surprised her then, reaching out to take one of her hands in his, holding it against the firmness of his thigh so she could feel the heat of him and the play of muscle through the cotton of his chinos. He gave her fingers a squeeze before returning his hand to the steering-wheel and it was a moment before she realised she had allowed her own fingers to linger on his thigh. Hastily, she snatched her hand back, disturbed by how much she wanted to touch him. All over.

'They'll love you,' he reassured her, voice low and husky. 'How can they not?'

She felt both warmed and unsettled by his words but she had no more time to dwell on them—or on her own salacious thoughts— because they were pulling into the gravelled drive of Conor and Kate's house. On the edge of the village and hidden from view by a high hedge, it was set back from the road and on a slight rise, allowing great views over the Solway Firth to the south and the Galloway hills to the north. Built of granite, the house was mostly long and low with a white-painted, two-storey addition at one end with a pitched slate roof and two chimneys. It was a gorgeous place, and even as she climbed out of the car she was admiring the large verdant garden stretching away from the house.

Before Francesca had time to catch her breath, Luke had taken her hand and was leading her forward. The front door opened before they reached it and a smiling woman, wearing a mulberry-coloured jersey dress, stepped out to greet them. In her mid-thirties, Francesca judged, Kate Anderson was beautiful. Her glossy walnut brown hair fell to her shoulders, while her dark brown eyes were warm with welcome.

'Luke, it's lovely to see you again.'

'You, too, Kate.'

Francesca felt a knot in her stomach as Kate kissed Luke on both cheeks and then turned to her with a smile, the unexpected hug taking her by surprise. 'And you must be Francesca. I'm so delighted to meet you and put a face to the name after all this time. Our patients always come back from the hospital after scans and X-rays saying how marvellous you have been and we appreciate that you take such good care of them.'

'Thank you,' Francesca managed, feeling overwhelmed, conscious of Luke stepping closer and resting a reassuring hand at the small of her back, as if he was aware how nervous she felt.

'Conor will be back shortly...he was called to see a patient. We were out late last night seeing friends—Kyle and Alexandra Sinclair. You might know of them, they work at the Rigtownbrae practice,' Kate added as an aside, and Francesca nodded, again recognising Kyle's name from hospital paperwork. Kate smiled and continued. 'Rebecca stayed with her grandparents. My dad retired up here and married Aileen, our practice manager. Conor is collecting Rebecca on his way home.'

'I'll sneak her present in now, then,' Luke decided, returning to the car and manoeuvring the huge plush elephant out after a bit of a struggle.

'Oh, my! It's twice the size of Rebecca!' Kate exclaimed. 'Where on earth are we going to hide it? The prof is an idiot!'

'It was his last act of revenge because he couldn't talk me out of leaving. Can you imagine how I felt, carrying this through the hospital from his office? I was teased mercilessly,' Luke moaned, pulling a face and making them both laugh.

'You poor thing! Still, Rebecca *is* going to adore it,' Kate admitted, giving the squishy trunk a squeeze. 'The trouble is she'll want to take it everywhere!'

Carrying the wine, flowers and present for Rebecca, Francesca followed Luke and Kate into the house. As she waited while a hiding place was found for the jumbo-sized jumbo, Luke's remark reminded her that she still hadn't discovered his third reason for giving up his promising career in London to return to Scotland.

Inside, the house proved to be just as lovely as the outside suggested, with a warm, welcoming feel. Kate, open and friendly, took them through to the large farmhouse kitchen and while their hostess, delighted with the gifts, put the flowers in a vase, both Francesca and Luke made a fuss of the Andersons' two beautiful grey cats, Smoky and Willow.

'So, how is the prof?' Kate asked a few moments later, pouring them each a glass of home-made lemonade and inviting them to sit at the scrubbed pine table. 'Terrorising the junior doctors as usual?'

'Absolutely. I was petrified when I first joined his team,' Luke admitted.

Kate chuckled. 'Me, too. Then you find out his bark is worse than his bite.'

'You must have tamed him.' Luke's smile was teasing. 'All we heard was Kate this and Kate that.'

'It'll be you now,' Kate riposted, teasing him back. 'You're the new golden boy and a whole new generation of junior doctors will have your example to live up to!'

Luke groaned. 'Don't.'

That Luke had been a rising star on Professor Fielding-Smythe's orthopaedic team hadn't escaped Francesca. The professor was a renowned, eminent surgeon with a reputation for being a hard taskmaster and someone who didn't suffer fools gladly. That he hadn't wanted Luke to leave said much about Luke's skill and promise. So why *had* Luke turned his back on London? What was it that had brought him back to Strathlochan?

She was pondering the question when the sound of another car arriving in the driveway outside announced the return of Conor and Rebecca. Once more the butterflies in Francesca's stomach took flight, increasing her nervousness. She glanced up as the back door opened and a handsome man of similar colouring to Luke stepped into the kitchen. He had an overnight bag and a teddy bear in one hand, while his other arm supported his daughter on his hip. The little girl's legs were wrapped around his waist as she clung to him like a limpet. Francesca could see straight away that Rebecca was a miniature copy of her mother. She was also shy. Seeing strangers in her home, she buried her face in her father's neck.

'Everything OK?' Kate asked, rising to her feet.

Smiling, Conor set the bag and bear down on the table, giving Kate a kiss before handing over their daughter. 'Fine.'

'Hi, pumpkin,' Kate greeted Rebecca, hugging the child before setting her down. 'Did you have a good time?'

Rebecca nodded, clinging to her mother's skirt and partially hiding behind her leg, watching with big, solemn eyes as Conor introduced himself.

'Hello, Luke, thanks for coming.' The two men shook hands and Francesca felt almost as shy as

Rebecca as Conor turned to her, taking her aback as he gave her a kiss on both cheeks. 'Welcome, Francesca. It's a pleasure to finally meet you.'

'And you,' she murmured politely.

Francesca had a few moments to pull herself together as Conor quizzed Luke on his car…something about it being voted top in the Green Awards for low carbon emissions and good fuel economy.

'Boys and their toys,' Kate murmured, rolling her eyes. 'Come on through, Francesca, and let me show you the rest of the house. I'm sure Conor will call us when the food is ready.'

'It'll be ten minutes,' her husband confirmed, checking the oven before setting about laying the table, surprising Francesca that he should be responsible for cooking what smelled like a delicious lunch.

'I only married Conor for his fish pie,' Kate confided, leading her out of the kitchen.

Conor's response followed them. 'I heard that. I think I have one or two other talents you appreciate,' he called suggestively, making Kate blush and laugh again.

Francesca enjoyed her tour of the beautiful house, but a short time later they returned to the kitchen and took their places at the table. Rebecca sat on a booster cushion next to her father, still silent as she made up her mind about the strangers.

'This is amazing,' Francesca praised after her first couple of mouthfuls of the wonderful fish pie.

Kate grinned. 'I told you!'

'You'll have to give me the recipe, Conor,' Luke suggested, and Francesca felt warm at the intimate look he sent her. 'I got lazy when Ma was staying with me in London as she insisted on doing the cooking while I was working. Living alone after she returned to Strathlochan, I've been slowly widening my repertoire.'

Knowing that Luke had lived alone and that there was no woman pining for him in London brought far too much relief and satisfaction. Alarmed at the direction of her thoughts, Francesca was relieved when the conversation moved on.

'How is Annie doing?' Kate asked.

'Very well,' Francesca was delighted to reply. 'She's hoping to get back to work soon. At the moment she and Nathan are away on holiday. They took up the invitation to stay for a week at Seb Adriani's family villa on Elba.'

'How lovely! We met Seb and Gina through

Nic and Hannah in Lochanrig,' Kate explained, confirming once more how close-knit the medical community was in the area.

'You were there when Annie was hurt, weren't you, Francesca?' Conor queried, helping Rebecca with her drink. 'It must have been frightening.'

She met Luke's gaze and noted his concern. 'Yes, it was at the time. Nathan was wonderful and saved Annie's life, keeping her with us until the senior consultant on duty, Robert Mowbray, could do the emergency thoracotomy.'

They talked about the incident for a while and then about Seb and Gina's upcoming wedding in May, which led on to talk about Conor and Kate's honeymoon. Rebecca wriggled off her chair and went to the fridge, proudly pointing out the photos, stuck on with magnets, of the orphaned elephant they had heard so much about.

Francesca was amazed how quickly the time went and she found herself relaxing. Rebecca, having overcome her initial shyness, chattered away, charming them all. As they moved to the sitting room after lunch, the little girl gravitated to Luke, climbing onto his lap, giggling as he teased her gently and tickled her.

Seeing Luke with Rebecca pulled at Francesca's heartstrings and tugged at some previously unknown maternal thread inside her. She hadn't thought about children, had not imagined she would have them. A relationship had never been in her plans. And her mother, devoid of any nurturing gene, had hardly been the ideal role model. Looking at him with the little girl, she knew instinctively that Luke would be an amazing father. A sudden longing curled deep within her, scaring her. She was getting in too deep. Alarmed at the direction of her thoughts, she excused herself and escaped to the bathroom, giving herself a stern lecture while she was there.

When she returned to the living room a short while later, the French doors were open. Kate was nowhere in sight, while Luke and Conor were outside, kicking a ball around with Rebecca on the lawn. Francesca stepped onto the patio to watch them.

'Two fine men we have there,' Kate commented, coming to stand beside her.

Uncomfortable, Francesca sought to set the record straight. 'Luke and I are friends.' As she said the words, she wondered who she was trying to convince…Kate or herself.

'Forgive me if I'm speaking out of turn, but as someone who was once so adamant that I didn't need anyone and was convinced I wanted to be alone, don't be too hasty in dismissing what you and Luke have together.'

'Kate…'

'I know, it isn't my business. But whatever you may think now, there's something special between you,' she said, sincerity in her words. 'I can see it just watching you. Luke really cares for you.'

'We're old friends,' Francesca repeated, but even as she spoke she knew something far more simmered beneath the surface, something hot and raw and exciting—but unacknowledged, at least by her.

Kate rested a hand on her arm, the expression in her brown eyes revealing her understanding. 'It's scary at first, but you won't regret taking the plunge.'

'I don't know.'

'I've been through a lot in the past, and I know how easy it is to keep people at arm's length, that it feels safer than ever trusting anyone again. But when it's right, it is so worth taking that leap of faith. All I'm saying is give Luke— and yourself—a chance,' her new friend advised. 'Don't make the mistake I so nearly did and throw away something rare and wonderful. I nearly lost Conor because I didn't believe…not in myself or my right to be happy…but thankfully he did and he refused to give up on me. He's the best thing that's ever happened to me, Francesca. Luke could be the same for you. When it's the right person, your fears fade away.'

Unsure what to say, Francesca remained silent, thankful when Kate moved back into the house. Alone once more, she watched as Conor and Luke reduced Rebecca to breathless laughter. There were similarities between the two men, but Conor's moss-green eyes were darker than Luke's, and while their hair was the same shade, Luke's was longer, more rakish and tousled. Luke was also two or three inches taller than Conor, although both shared an athletic build, strong and leanly muscled.

Conor was laid-back with an easygoing nature and ready humour. That he and Kate were deeply in love was obvious from every look and every touch. Francesca felt a peculiar sense of envy. She'd never wanted to be close to anyone, but seeing Conor and Kate together stirred something within her. As did interacting with Rebecca. Those previously dormant maternal instincts were slowly awakening in the little girl's presence, confusing her even more.

As for Luke, in character he was much more complex than Conor. There was a hint of danger about him, an air of the bad boy that Francesca had always been attracted to, an edge that called to everything feminine inside her, tempting the repressed good girl she had been in her teens to rebel.

Her musings were cut short as Kate returned to the patio with a tray of tea. She set it on the table and called the others to join them. Francesca sat down, enjoying the views down to the Solway Firth, pleased it was warm enough for them to sit outside. Rebecca came running up, taking a long drink of her milk before setting her beaker back on the table. Francesca smiled as the girl turned to face her.

'I love your hair,' Rebecca told her, moving closer.

'Thank you. Yours is beautifully shiny, like your mother's.'

Rebecca nodded, nibbling her lip. 'Can I touch it?'

'OK.' Taken aback, she looked up, finding Luke watching her as he stood in the garden with Conor.

Luke watched as Rebecca talked to Francesca. The child seemed fascinated with Francesca's hair, taking a strand in her fingers, straightening it and letting go, giggling as it sprang back into its wayward corkscrew curl again. Not that he blamed Rebecca. That wild mass of fiery flame fascinated him, too, and he longed to run his fingers through it, to feel it against his skin, to see it spread out in wild abandon across his pillow.

'You OK?' Conor asked, resting a hand on his shoulder.

'Yeah.' He nodded but didn't take his gaze off Francesca. 'I was just imagining half a dozen little Chessie replicas with clouds of red hair and big grey eyes,' he admitted, glancing at Conor. 'You're very lucky.'

The other man nodded, his own gaze on Kate. 'And I know it, believe me. I give thanks every day. So, what's the story with you and Francesca?' he asked after a reflective pause.

'We knew each other at school. Our backgrounds were very different but we both had family issues, were both loners who sort of gravitated together. Chessie was bullied a lot and I tried to step in and watch over her. Then circumstances parted us and I lost track of her when she moved away,' he explained, telling Conor how his mother's freak accident had led to the discovery that Francesca had returned to Strathlochan.

'So you left the prof's team and came rushing back.'

'I did,' he admitted with a wry chuckle, knowing how foolish his actions must seem to others. 'Part of me knows it was crazy. We'd not seen each other in ten years. I'd only kissed her once. But I just know deep inside that it's right.'

'Then you did the best thing,' Conor confirmed, understanding and supportive.

Luke was silent for a moment, watching Francesca, knowing how nervous she had been. It was so good to see her relaxed and enjoying herself. 'The tough job is breaking through her barriers and persuading her we're better together than we are apart.'

'Been there, got the T-shirt.' Conor smiled and they started walking back to join the others on the patio. 'Don't give up, Luke. Believe me, it's worth the effort.'

Conor's advice boosted his morale. Watching Conor with Kate and Rebecca made him envious. He wanted what they had. And he wanted it with Francesca.

It was early evening before they left the Andersons' home, turning down an invitation to stay for dinner because they had to be at work the next morning and Luke knew Francesca didn't want to be late back. After protracted goodbyes, because Rebecca was sorry to see them leave, they set off along the country lanes towards Strathlochan. Francesca seemed content to doze, so Luke took some moments alone with his thoughts to reflect on the last couple of days.

The time spent with Francesca at the rescue centre and walking in the grounds of Strathlochan Castle yesterday had been precious. He felt he knew so much more about the inner woman and all she had overcome. And he loved her for her passion for animals, especially the dogs. He'd fallen for them, too.

Today had been better than he'd hoped. Conor and Kate were an inspirational couple. He'd been affected by spending time with them, and he could only hope that experiencing their home and relationship at close quarters would convince Francesca that the way they had grown up was unusual. Conor's support had encouraged him and seeing the young family had whetted his appetite for a happy home of his own.

As they were approaching Strathlochan, he woke Francesca up. 'Hey, sleepyhead,' he said, reaching out to give her shoulder a gentle shake.

'Hi,' she murmured after a moment, slowly opening her eyes and sitting up straight. 'Where are we?'

'Nearly back home. Do you want to stop and pick up some food?'

She shook her head, causing her curls to shimmer like licks of flame. 'I'm not sure I can eat much more after that lovely lunch. I have some salad in the fridge.'

'OK.'

Taking that as an invitation, whether she had meant it as one or not, Luke drove back to Francesca's flat. He followed her inside, helping her assemble a salad with some cold chicken, adding rocket, watercress, tomato, cucumber and a few other bits before putting some coffee on to brew while she gathered plates, cutlery and glasses.

'Thanks for coming with me today,' he said when they sat to eat their meal.

'I enjoyed it.' He heard the surprise and edge of confusion in her voice and hid a smile. 'They're nice people.'

Luke nodded. 'They are. Rebecca's going to break a lot of hearts when she grows up.'

'Kate says Conor has decreed Rebecca's not allowed to date until she's thirty!'

Her laugh was infectious and good to hear. Luke joined in, knowing he'd feel as protective as Conor if he was lucky enough to have daughters with Francesca. Their meal over, knowing it was a risk but needing to move things on and lead up to asking her about next weekend, Luke angled his chair so he was facing her.

'You don't date much. Why?' he asked, sensing her tension as she looked away, shrugging her shoulders.

'I'm busy with work.' She flicked him a quick glance and retreated again. 'Besides, I've never looked for a relationship. I'm better on my own.'

He frowned. Although this was what he'd suspected, he ached for her aloneness, and knew the challenge he would face to gain acceptance into her life. 'And sex?'

'I'm not a virgin, if that's what you mean.'

Thank goodness—or she'd be shocked stupid by the things he wanted to do with her. Not that he told her that. Yet. The boldness of her words were not matched by the tone of her voice or the expression in her silver-grey eyes. He wasn't fooled for a moment by her tough-girl act. And while the thought of any other man touching her made him wild with jealousy, he'd bet a whole lot that her experience hadn't been great because she certainly didn't radiate the aura of a well-satisfied woman, taken to the heights of pleasure from long hours of loving. Not now. But he hoped that she would before too much longer. This time he did smile, he couldn't help it, imagining her begging him to take her to places she'd never been before.

'What's funny?' she demanded, rising to her feet and setting the plates noisily on the drainer, her temper obvious.

'Nothing, Chessie.' He moved next to her and slid a hand along the creamy smooth skin of her neck, the pad of his thumb picking up the acceleration of her pulse at her throat. 'I can assure you that I'm taking this very seriously.'

He felt her swallow. 'Luke…'

'I know you feel the chemistry between us.'

Indecision clouded her eyes but he forced himself to wait. It had taken all the patience he possessed to go slowly these last days when all he had wanted was to sweep her up in his arms and make love to her with everything in him, to bind her to him for ever. She was skittish, he knew about the issues of the past, and he didn't want to rush her, but his patience only stretched so far. He thought of Conor's advice and knew he had to play this carefully, pressing her forward but not so far she bolted.

'Tell me what's worrying you,' he coaxed, lowering his voice, his thumb soothing slow circles on her silky skin, stepping closer so he could breathe in her subtle flowery fragrance. 'What's scaring you about exploring what we have?'

'I don't do relationships. And I don't want to lose your friendship,' she admitted after another long pause, her voice unsteady.

He tilted her chin up so he could look into her eyes—so she could look into his and see that he meant what he said. 'You'll *never* lose me, Chessie. But I would like more than friendship. I want us to be together.'

'How do you know it won't spoil everything?'

'How do you know it will?' he countered, knowing she had fears he'd yet to fully understand but desperate to set them to rest.

She shook her head as if at a loss for a reply.

'I care about you, Chessie,' he told her, keeping back the full extent of his feelings so he didn't pressure her too much. 'We have so much in common. We don't trust many people, but we trust each other. We're independent. We understand each other and what we faced—from inside the home and outside it— as no one else can. We never fit in with other people, not totally, yet we're right together. We've both come back here to prove to ourselves that we can...and to show others that we made it.'

Everything Luke said was true. Their roots may have grown in different soil but once above the surface they had faced similar conditions in terms of weathering the ostracism and neglect. Throughout it all, as unusual as their association had been, they'd had each other...until Luke had left. No matter how much she told herself otherwise, she'd never forgotten him, had thought about him all the time throughout the ten long years since she had last seen him.

Now he had returned and working with him, spending time with him, had brought back all the old feelings, not as some innocent teenager with her first crush but as a woman for a man. He was mature, potently masculine, still as kind, but dangerously exciting. And he tempted her more than any man had ever done. Not that she'd had much experience. Her liaisons had been very few and very unsatisfactory. No way was she telling Luke she'd never found sex pleasurable. But if there *was* something wrong with her—the Ice Maiden—how come she responded to Luke?

Her flesh burned from his touch as he trailed one fingertip across the scooped neckline of her top, dipping down to teasingly whisper across the upper swell of her breasts, jolting her from her reverie. 'W-what are you doing?'

'Mmm?' The sexy drawl, lazy and husky, threatened to liquefy her bones. Thick lashes lifted slowly and lanquid green eyes looked into hers. 'I have a thing about your freckles.'

'My freckles are horrid,' she protested breathlessly, startled by his appreciation of what had been the bane of her life. She feared she lost all will and common sense when he was so close to her.

'No, they're not. I love them. I want to find and count and kiss each one.'

A tremor shuddered through her at the very thought of Luke's sinful mouth and wicked hands travelling all over her body. How could she feel as she did when he looked at her or touched her when no other man had ever roused any kind of response in her? She shouldn't let Luke take things further. But how could she resist the charge of sexual energy between them? No matter what he said, she feared all would be lost if they made love. What if she couldn't handle a relationship?

She couldn't understand how she could feel so safe and comfortable with Luke and yet so nervous and uncertain at the same time. He was the person she felt closest to and yet a part of her deep inside felt threatened by him because she knew she could all too easily come to care too deeply for him, to depend on him, to lose herself in him. And she couldn't afford to do that. The lessons were deeply ingrained to remain alone, to not need anyone, to retain control. The temptation to need Luke was so strong it frightened her.

Yet however stupid it sounded, hadn't some secret part of her always felt Luke was her destiny, that they had always been meant to be together? She thought of Kate, of her encouragement to take a leap of faith and jump into the unknown and allow Luke to catch her. Could she do it? Could she afford *not* to do it?

'You think too much, Chessie.'

Luke's warm palms cupped her face and all thought vanished as his lips brushed hers, teasing, tormenting. An involuntary whimper escaped, her mouth opening under his in a blatant invitation he accepted at once, deepening the kiss, driving her crazy with his taste, his heat, with the promise of all that could follow. He was addictive. She couldn't get close enough. But nothing she did helped to ease the terrible burning ache of need inside her, an ache that was unfamiliar and urgent.

Luke's hands grazed down her body, leaving a trail of fire in their wake, but that was nothing compared to the explosion of flaming need as he inched up her skirt until his fingers had free access to the bare skin of her thighs. She moaned into his mouth, her hands clutching his shoulders as she tried to steady herself, her knees too weak to hold her up, the explosion of sensations over-whelming her.

As his lips left hers, she drew in a ragged breath, intoxicated by the musky masculine scent of him. He nibbled around the line of her jaw while his exploring fingers rose higher and higher up her legs, teasing and caressing, tight-ening the needy ache inside her until she thought she would explode. Her whole body quivered in response as he sucked on her earlobe, his words husky and outrageous and unbearably arousing.

'I want you, Chessie. I want to kiss you all over, to taste you and explore every part of you. I want to watch you come apart as I make love to you,' he told her in a rough whisper, making love to her now with his words, his voice. 'I want to watch you as you take me deep inside you and feel you wrap around me, as we share our pleasure.'

Somehow she froze and melted at the same time, feeling her breasts tighten and the throb between her legs intensify. How could he, with a few deft touches and a few naughty words, make her feel things she had never experienced before? 'Luke,' she moaned, confused and surprised, pressing her thighs together to make it stop.

'That won't make it go away,' he tormented.

As if he knew exactly what he was doing to her and how she was feeling, he moved one hand to massage low over the ache, driving her crazy with impatience. 'Open for me.' The whispered words were impossible to ignore and she bit her lip to hold back her sob as her thighs shamelessly parted of their own volition. 'Let me do this for you, Chessie. Let me give you pleasure and show you how magical it's going to be.'

His mouth was hot on her throat, his tongue learning the hollow, pressing over the spot where her pulse raced out of control, his teeth nipping her skin as his hand slid inside her panties. This time she couldn't halt the sob that was torn from her as his fingers began a devastating invasion, stroking, teasing, driving her to madness. She cried out, one hand closing on his wrist, not sure if she was trying to stop him or encourage him to go on for ever. It felt scary to be out of control. But the steady rise of pleasure was wonderful. His clever fingers incited, teased, inflamed, explored. Two eased inside her. A moan ripped from her as he found the sweetest of spots, and ruthlessly exploited it, stroking a rhythmic tempo that sent her into a frenzy.

'Is it good, Chessie?' he whispered hotly.

'Yes, yes! Oh, please, Luke…' She sagged against him, her hips moving to his touch. Sensations she had never known overwhelmed her, and she sobbed again as the pad of his thumb circled her clitoris, driving her to the point of no return, making her desperate for release. 'Luke! Please!'

His throaty chuckle was sexy against her ear as he sucked on her lobe. 'Do you like that?'

She couldn't speak, could do nothing but feel. Her head fell back, her body boneless, crying out again as she gave herself up to the strongest, most amazing experience she'd ever had…and the first mind-numbing orgasm of her life.

Aftershocks rippled through her, catching her unawares. When, finally, she was able to drag heavy-lidded eyes open, she saw the wicked smile curving Luke's sexy mouth. She was all too aware of him supporting her, and of his hand lingering, gentling her down to earth again before he adjusted her clothes back into place. Embarrassed colour tinged her cheeks as she recalled her wild abandonment and she tried to hide her face from him, burying it in his chest, breathing in his scent.

'Don't,' he admonished softly. 'It was beautiful, Chessie. *You're* beautiful. And I want to give you even more pleasure. Just think how good it's going to be for us when we really make love.' Her pulse skyrocketed as her thoughts disobeyed her and did just that. 'Give me next weekend, Chessie,' he continued, his hands cradling her face. 'Come to my house. Stay with me. Let me show you how special it will be for us.' He pressed a finger to her lips to still her anxious protest. She found herself silenced as much by the vulnerability in his eyes as by his touch. 'Don't say anything now. We're on day shift from tomorrow until Friday, and then we're off for the weekend before starting nights on Monday. Spend that time with me before you dismiss us being together. Please.'

He kissed her once more with exquisite gentleness and heartfelt emotion before he stepped back. She looked deep into his eyes, seeing the passion, the need, the desire, the turmoil of uncertainty about her answer. And then he was gone.

As the front door closed behind him, Francesca leaned weakly against the kitchen counter, her whole body trembling and limp. Yes, she was more than attracted to Luke. But

she didn't want sex to spoil their friendship.
Luke believed they could have it all. But would
it work? She wouldn't know unless she tried.
But what if, in doing so, she lost the one person
she truly felt close to and could be herself with?

Francesca felt weighed down with uncertainty.
Could she take the risk?

She had five days to decide whether to say yes
or no.

CHAPTER SEVEN

'COME on in, Victoria, and take a seat,' Luke invited as his penultimate patient of Friday afternoon's fracture clinic came into the treatment room.

The notation system used on the front of files made for easy reference for any clinician accessing the case and the information told Luke that the nineteen-year-old had broken her collarbone a week ago in a fall from her mountain bike. There had been some displacement but not enough to cause concern. However, she had been referred back today for a check-up and a further X-ray to ensure that there had been no further movement and that the bone was stable and beginning to heal.

'How have things been? Are you having any pain?' he asked as Victoria sat down, observing how careful the slim blonde was of her left arm, which was supported in a sling.

'It's still very sore at night, which makes it hard to sleep. I can't get comfortable,' the girl admitted with a grimace, dark circles under her blue eyes. 'During the day, if I keep it still it's OK but any movement is tender. Thankfully Francesca was very gentle when she took the X-ray just now and it didn't hurt too much.'

'That's good.'

Just hearing Francesca's name was enough to stir Luke's blood and cause his mind to wander, not helped when the intercom buzzed and her melodious, softly accented voice informed him that Victoria's images were ready.

'Would you like me to bring them in?' she asked.

'Please, Francesca.'

It wasn't necessary as he could view the digital pictures on the computer screen, but he had come to value Francesca's opinion, impressed with the way she spotted things other people missed. Besides, it was one more excuse to see her and be close to her for a few moments.

As always around the hospital, he was careful to keep things professional when Francesca arrived and together they viewed the details of the fracture and kept their patient updated on her progress. Luke carried out a short examination of the shoulder and movement, apologetic when the young woman winced.

'These can be very difficult injuries to treat, Victoria,' Luke explained to the girl as he sat down again and faced her. 'It's an awkward position and, unlike an arm or a leg, we can't put it in a cast. Your latest X-rays show that the ends of the bone have not moved, there is no displacement and no operation or pinning is necessary.'

'I see.'

Hearing the young woman's disappointment, he gave her a sympathetic smile. 'I know it isn't easy but it's healing well and I'm afraid the only thing we can do is wait it out. It can take a while to mend. Keep the sling on for at least another two weeks to keep your shoulder supported. But it's also important to maintain movement in your hand, wrist and elbow. We can arrange some physiotherapy exercises for you and you can gradually build up strength as the tenderness eases,' he finished, knowing some patients became frustrated when the healing seemed slow.

'Shall I keep on taking the pills I was given?'

the young woman queried, handing him the pack with the remaining blister strips enclosed.

'I think you should stop them if they're not helping you. Are you taking medication for anything else?' Victoria shook her head and Luke paused a moment, considering. The tenderness should be easing but clearly sleep was a problem and he decided to change Victoria's prescription, keying an instruction into the computer. 'I've written you up for something different that should help make you more comfortable at night.'

Victoria's relief was evident. 'Thank you. I must admit the continual ache has been getting me down.'

'I'm not surprised. Let's hope the change in medication will help ease that. We'll make an appointment for you to come back in a fortnight and we'll review things again then. In the meantime, contact us or your GP if you have any worries or queries.'

'Thank you, Mr Devlin. And you, Francesca,' she added, rising to her feet and taking the new prescription Luke handed her as it emerged from the printer. 'You've both been really kind.'

As Francesca accompanied the young woman out, Luke was left alone for a few moments with his jumbled thoughts. Chief amongst them remained the fear that even after the erotic moments they had shared in Francesca's kitchen on Sunday night, she would still turn him down. He hadn't meant things to go as far as they had but he hadn't been able to stop when she had responded to him so openly and with such sensual enthusiasm. It hadn't mattered that his body had ached and his own needs had remained unfulfilled…all important had been ensuring Francesca's total enjoyment and abandoned pleasure. The unrestrained evidence of her desire and her uninhibited climax had been reward enough. For now. Just thinking about her, seeing her, hearing her voice or remembering how she had responded to his touch was enough to make him hot and hard. He'd never taken so many cold showers as he had this last couple of weeks.

Francesca's reactions and her shocked delight at her release had confirmed what he had already suspected…that despite her chin-up defensive words that she was not a virgin, sexually fulfilling experiences were uncommon for her. It gave him a rush of possessive gratification that no one else had made love to her properly—or ever would if he had his way. *He* wanted to be the one to show Francesca everything, to indulge her happiness, to introduce her to real pleasure and to be the one to give her total satisfaction.

He hadn't been a monk for ten years. He'd had needs like anyone else, but he'd met them rarely, and only with women who had wanted nothing more from their brief associations than he had. There had only ever been one woman with whom he wanted a meaningful relationship, to whom he intended to commit himself heart and body and soul—and that was Francesca. If she would let him. And therein lay the crux of his anxiety and uncertainty.

As the clinic nurse popped her head round the door to announce that Francesca was with Mr Mitchell, their final patient of the day, Luke thanked her and forced himself to focus back on work. After writing up Victoria's notes, he turned his attention to reviewing Hector Mitchell's file. A frown creased his brow as he read the seventy-two-year-old's long and complicated history, knowing he could trust Francesca to be taking the necessary series of X-rays and scans he would need to assess the man's current condition after he had fallen at home.

A while later the door opened again and when he glanced up this time, it was Francesca herself who came back into the room. 'Hi,' he greeted her, unable to help his voice dropping to a husky tone as it always seemed to when he was with her.

'Hi.'

Long dusky lashes shaded her grey eyes and hid her expression as she closed the door and moved into the room, but her smile, though fleeting, warmed him, making it hard to hold on to the patience he had fought so hard to maintain all week.

A long, long week during which he had been determined to act in the same way as always and to show Francesca how much her friendship mattered to him—which meant not pressuring her or doing anything to influence her as she made her decision about this weekend. But waiting was killing him. If she said no, what was he going to do? Giving up was not an option, not with so much at stake.

Most people would think he was crazy, being so fixated on Francesca when they'd not seen each other in ten years, yet he could not explain how he knew deep inside…had *always* known…

that the connection between them, born so young and in such difficult circumstances, was special and right and lifelong. He cared little what other people thought. What mattered was Francesca and her feelings. He wasn't arrogant enough to think it would be easy, or to take her for granted, which was why he was so nervous.

If he hadn't considered just how deeply Francesca's fears of losing control might run before he returned to Strathlochan, he certainly understood now. He'd taken a big risk. He needed her as much as he needed his next breath. Somehow he had to convince her to give them a chance. She was a loner. So was he. But together they worked…were stronger, better in every way. He had pinned everything on doing all he could to prove that to her, to calm her fears and to have Francesca share his dream of the future—a future that saw them together, bonded in every way, as friends *and* as lovers.

If he couldn't…

Doubts gnawed away inside him. Not least among them what Francesca would say when she saw his house. A house he had bought as an investment, or so he told the outside world, but the purchase had been made with his heart and not his head, clinging to an old remembered dream and a hope for a future that might never be fulfilled. Now that dream—the fantasy of sharing his woodland cottage with Francesca and a few children—might not be so far-fetched. But he had an uphill battle ahead, breaking through her defences and combating her lifetime of conditioning. She seemed to think that friendship and a relationship were incompatible, that if they made love, the friendship would end. She couldn't be more wrong. But how to convince her of that? And how, if she *did* say yes to this weekend, could he bear if it she walked away afterwards and wanted nothing more from him?

Before he could find any answers to those questions, they had to discuss Mr Mitchell. As he had not seen the man before, he asked Francesca's views, immediately noting her tension, the annoyance and edginess she was trying to hide.

'What's wrong, Chessie?'

She shook her head, her gaze down, her fingers toying with the case file. 'As he's the last patient of the day, I thought you might see Mr Mitchell in the other room. He's uncomfortable and I didn't think it fair to make him move again to come in here.'

'That's fine,' Luke agreed, knowing she was stalling and hiding something. 'Tell me what's bothering you. Is it Mr Mitchell?'

His half plea, half instruction brought a sigh from her. 'In a roundabout way. I've just had a run-in with wretched Olivia,' she finally admitted.

'How delightful,' he responded sardonically. He'd scarcely been at the hospital a day before Olivia had literally hunted him down and come on to him, as Francesca had predicted, but he had set her straight in no uncertain terms about his lack of interest in her personally and about what he thought of her treatment of his mother. The trauma nurse had wisely given him a wide berth since. 'What's she done now?'

'Luke…'

As Francesca bit her lip, her reticence and discomfort alerted him to this being something he wouldn't like. 'What happened?'

'It's nothing.'

'It must be something or you wouldn't be upset,' he pointed out, knowing Francesca was not one to overreact.

'After Victoria left, I went to call Mr Mitchell and discovered Olivia talking to him and his wife,' she explained, anger making her grey eyes steely. 'Olivia has no business being near the clinic. Anyway, she scuttled off when she saw me. I asked Mr and Mrs Mitchell if everything was all right and…'

As Francesca paused again, Luke leaned forward, folding his arms on the desk. 'And? Tell me,' he encouraged.

'It seems that Olivia was trying to sow seeds of doubt in the Mitchells' minds.'

'About what?' he persisted.

'About you.' He noted how Francesca hands clenched into fists, although her voice was carefully controlled. 'Olivia had made comments about your family—apparently one of your brothers once burgled their home years ago.'

Banking the fury that flared inside him, Luke rose to his feet, unable to rid his body of the tension that gripped him and the bitter resentment of how the past he couldn't change refused to release him from its hold.

'Well, it's true I'm a Devlin—or a Devil'n as people liked to play with the name. They all thought we'd been spawned by Satan himself.'

'Don't, Luke,' Francesca protested, closing the gap between them and laying her hand on his arm, making him feel as if a zing of electricity had coursed through him at her touch. 'You know that's not true. Only a handful are small-minded enough to believe that, and Olivia has her own agenda for causing trouble.'

Francesca's anger at Olivia was evident as she chided him, ever loyal and staunch in her support of him, just as she had been when they'd been youngsters. 'I presume the Mitchells want to see another surgeon. I can call someone else to take the case.'

'Of course not.'

Francesca's reply shocked him. 'They don't?'

'No.' There was a feisty expression in her eyes. 'Nina Mitchell might look like a frail bird in stature, but she's strong in temperament, just like her husband. Neither of them were prepared to pay Olivia any heed—especially when they were made aware of your qualifications.'

'You said something to them.'

It was obvious by the slight flush that pinkened freckle-dusted, ivory cheeks that Francesca had spoken up for him…again. 'I just explained your skill as an orthopaedic surgeon and pointed out that you couldn't be held responsible for the actions of someone else, related or not, that happened years ago. Mr Mitchell is happy to see you—if you don't mind coming to the other room. I left the nurse with them and she's making Mrs Mitchell a cup of tea.'

Luke wanted to kiss her. Not because she had smoothed things over with the Mitchells, or because she was angry on his behalf, but because she believed in him without question. As Francesca turned for the door, he caught her hand.

'Just a minute. What about Olivia?'

'You should report her—I know the Mitchells are going to—and goodness knows what she's saying to other people. It isn't right!' she exclaimed, bristling with indignation.

Luke had every intention of taking care of Nurse Barr's loose tongue but that wasn't the primary concern on his mind at the moment. 'I meant between you. You said you'd had a run-in with her,' he reminded her, intrigued by the way her flush deepened and she looked swiftly away from him…but not before he caught the guilty embarrassment in her eyes.

'I just advised her not to make any more wild accusations or tell lies to patients,' she admitted after a moment's pause, but he could tell from her edginess there was more to the story.

'And?' he pressed as she fidgeted, holding on

to her hand when she would have pulled away to put more distance between them.

'Olivia made certain…comments.'

He raised an eyebrow. 'Comments?'

'Yes.' Francesca's embarrassment increased. 'About you and her.'

'There has never been, and will never be, anything between me and Olivia,' he was swift to state, surprised by the sudden giggle she tried to stifle.

'I know.'

She wouldn't look at him and his suspicions increased. He caught her chin and tilted her face up, trying to look stern as he studied her. 'Francesca, what have you done?'

'I didn't mean anything by it, she just got me so mad, making snide remarks about how I was the laughing stock of the hospital in the way I was apparently throwing myself at you,' she began, her brow knitted in annoyance.

Luke tried desperately not to laugh. She looked so cute. And nothing would delight him more than that she throw herself at him, but he knew how Olivia's baiting and mention of being the subject of hospital gossip would upset and unsettle Francesca.

'I'm really sorry, Luke,' she continued, clearly disturbed and agitated.

'Why apologise to me?'

'Because I stupidly drew you into the argument. I should have ignored her but knowing what Olivia is like and how she talks about all the men she's beguiled and how physically perfect they have to be to hold her interest, I'm afraid my temper got the better of me when she lied about having...relations with you.'

She huffed out a breath and he tweaked a strand of flame red hair, knowing that real explosions might be rare but when Francesca let go, woe betide her opponent. 'So what did you say?'

'When she was spouting off about me, the Ice Maiden, never being good enough for a man like you, especially being second best to her, I...' Another hesitation followed and she hung her head. 'I said it was good to know she had changed so much and hadn't let your unsightly birthmark put her off.'

As her words trailed off, Luke could hold his laughter back no longer. 'Chessie, you are priceless!' he managed when he could speak, ignoring her frown and hugging her close for a moment. 'I wonder how long it will be before word gets round the hospital that I'm flawed and have a birth defect?' he teased, laughing again as she groaned and pushed away from him.

'Don't joke about it. I'm sorry.'

'Forget it. The only one who will look stupid is Olivia,' he reassured her.

'I'm the stupid one. I know what they all say about me.' Shaking her head, she picked up the file from the desk. 'Come on, we can't keep Mr Mitchell waiting any longer.'

As he followed her from the room, he just managed to refrain from suggesting that tonight he would be happy for her to check him all over for any imperfections. And that they could really give the hospital gossipmongers something to talk about. But it was the wrong time and the wrong place. And Francesca was too edgy. For now he had to focus on the problem of Hector Mitchell's troubles.

All too soon their shift would be over. Then he would accompany her back to her flat and learn of her decision. Would she come home with him…or not?

As always when Francesca observed Luke with a patient, she could not help but be impressed with his manner and his skill. She knew how much Olivia's interference had upset him, and how embarrassed he felt at the news that one of his brothers had once done harm to this sweet elderly couple. But he had introduced himself with his usual courtesy and charm, offering them the option of seeing a different doctor if that would make them more comfortable, and his obvious emotion and gratitude when the Mitchells had given him their wholehearted confidence had been touching to see.

Now Francesca offered Nina Mitchell silent support as Luke examined her husband. She didn't know how many times Hector Mitchell had been through the radiology unit since her return to Strathlochan, but enough that she felt a special affinity with him and his wife. Today she had taken up-to-date images of the elderly man's sacrum and lumbar spine and she knew what Luke would be seeing. An old injury to the second lumbar vertebrae, which had collapsed some time ago. Despite his continued pain and problems, the basic alignment was generally good.

As Luke continued his gentle examination, inspection of the images and talked in detail to

Hector, Francesca found herself thinking back over the last week. A week in which all she had been able to do was think about Luke. Each night and often during the day she found herself reliving those incredible moments in her kitchen on Sunday night when Luke had introduced her to the kind of pleasure she had never believed she could experience.

She had long thought that she wasn't particularly sexual. Her two previous encounters, while she had been living in Edinburgh, had been brief and all about the man's pleasure and not her own. She hadn't been able to let go, to relax, but with Luke, whom she trusted and with whom she felt safe, it had been so different. Just thinking about his touch made her all hot and bothered. She had never had an orgasm before. That she had on Sunday night was all because of Luke. He'd been so unselfish, taking nothing for himself. Indeed, he'd said giving her pleasure was important and enjoyable for him.

This week she had seen Luke every day at work. Most evenings she had spent time with him, going for walks, out for meals, acting just as they had before last Sunday night. He had never once referred to the weekend, had never pressured her to make a decision, had never behaved any differently towards her or altered their friendship. It was to be entirely her choice. They kissed goodbye—less chaste kisses than in the beginning—but they never went over the edge into the cauldron of passion that bubbled just beneath the surface. She didn't know what it cost Luke to hold back, but she knew the terrible toll it took on her…the frustration, the longing, the confusion.

On Wednesday it had been his mother's birthday and Francesca had found herself spending the evening with Sadie and Luke, having a special dinner. Before eating, as it was the one night of the week the animal rescue centre stayed open later, they had taken Sadie to meet Sally. Sadie had met Murphy and Harry, making a big fuss of them, but the main reason for the visit had been for Sadie to adopt a cat. She had fallen for Freya, a beautiful young white female who was friendly and sweet-natured, but because she was deaf she needed a loving home, safe from road traffic. Sadie had taken one look at Freya and that had been it. With Freya equally contented to bond with Sadie, the match had been made and Sally had been delighted to sign the paperwork and for Sadie to take Freya home.

'Thank you for making this such a special birthday,' Sadie had told her as she had given her a hug before Francesca had left for home.

Moved and embarrassed, Francesca had smiled. 'It was my pleasure.'

'Your gift means a lot to me.' The older lady had looked at the cut-glass vase Francesca had chosen on advice from Luke with obvious pleasure. 'But your company was the best gift of all.' Sadie rested a palm against her cheek. 'You've turned into such a beautiful young woman, so kind and dedicated to your job. And thank you for making Luke so happy.'

Two days later and she was still thinking of Sadie's words and all the sentiments behind them. She remembered how many times, growing up, she had wished Sadie was her mother. It was the comment about her making Luke happy that had caused the most restless thought, however. Was it true? Sadie certainly thought so. If it was true, what did it mean? His return to Strathlochan, his friendship, just being with him had definitely changed her life and made her happier and more relaxed. But with those admissions came a flicker of unease…the acknowledgement that Luke had already come to mean a great deal to her. A complication she had not wanted in her life.

There was already gossip about them around the hospital, without the latest spiteful remarks from Olivia Barr, and Francesca knew Luke hated being the object of attention as much as she did. She was grateful that he always treated her professionally at work. He was always protective of her—just as he had been in their youth. Now, thanks to her own loss of temper, she had probably made things worse for them both.

As far as she could remember, there had been no rumours about Luke and girls at school. Lots of them had fancied the forbidden bad boy and had jockeyed for his attention but he had always ignored them because his focus had been on his work. Now she knew why. Like her, education had been Luke's way out. She had learned during their visit to the Andersons on Sunday that there had been no one special Luke had been seeing in London, but she couldn't imagine there hadn't been women in his life and it was ridiculous that she should feel jealous about it. She'd had no claim on him. And yet, however much she tried to deny it, deep inside a part of her felt she had always been his.

Which led back to her fears and her quandary about her decision. The week was nearly over and she had little time left to give Luke her answer.

'I would like the senior orthopaedic consultant, Maurice Goodwin, to see you, Mr Mitchell,' Luke was saying now, drawing Francesca's wayward attention back to work. 'There is no sign on the X-rays or scan that your fall has done any further damage, but I am concerned how long this situation has been going on.' He paused, careful to draw both husband and wife into the discussion, to listen to their questions and to fill them in on his thoughts. 'It may be possible for us to try another procedure to ease your discomfort and I'd like Mr Goodwin to discuss that with you. Is that all right?'

'We'd be really grateful,' Nina Mitchell admitted. 'For so long we've just felt we're never getting anywhere. Not that people haven't been kind, but we see a different doctor every time and no one seems to have an answer.'

Luke nodded, his sympathetic understanding evident. 'I'll talk to Mr Goodwin myself,' he promised them, making a note in his diary and on the file. 'We'll arrange an appointment as soon as possible and I'll make sure that I'm there, as well as Mr Goodwin. In the meantime, I've checked your notes and, with your discomfort increasing, I'm going to give you some stronger painkillers and a different non-steroidal anti-inflammatory drug.'

'Thank you, the discomfort is wearing me down,' Hector confided, emotion making his voice unsteady.

'Let's hope these new drugs will help.' Luke carefully helped the elderly man to readjust his clothes and then rise to his feet with the aid of his walking stick before settling into his electric-powered wheelchair. 'If you have any problems or questions, or any effects from the change in pills that worries you, ring me here at the hospital or contact your GP.'

Hector shook Luke's hand. 'We'll do that. Thank you so much.'

'And don't take any mind of what that awful nurse said, young man,' Nina offered forcefully. 'You've been excellent and we'll tell the hospital management so when we complain about her.'

'I'm just here to help you.' Luke smiled modestly but Francesca could see he was pleased.

She held the door open for the couple, watching for a moment as they made their way slowly down the corridor towards the exit.

'Do you think there *is* anything else you can do for him?' she asked Luke, tidying up the room while he finished writing up the notes.

'I hope so.' He closed the file and sat back, watching her. 'I've observed the prof do several procedures that have improved the quality of life for patients with symptoms the same as Mr Mitchell's. I'm hoping Maurice will agree to investigate it and give it a try.'

Her chores finished, Francesca went to the locker room to change while Luke returned the notes for filing and then did the same. Once more her stomach filled with fluttering butterflies. Not long now before she had to make her decision. She'd never been one to confide in people or been close enough to friends to ask for advice, but just for a moment she wished Annie was around so she could talk to her. But Annie and Nathan would not be back from Italy until the next day. And she had mere minutes now to make her choice.

With Luke she had already had a taste of an unimagined paradise. With him she knew she would experience the ultimate in pleasure. She trusted him—but did she trust herself? Twice when she had been living in Edinburgh, young, lonely and confused, she had made regrettable mistakes and had succumbed to meaningless sex. Now, just once, she longed to know what it was like to make love with someone special, someone who meant something, whose touch set her on fire.

But if she said yes and spent this weekend with Luke, would she survive it? How could she ever walk away? Because she could never give up control of herself. Not again. It was ingrained in her to be alone. Would being with Luke be a form of surrender? And what of their friendship? Was he right? Could it endure whatever happened? Because she didn't want to lose that. Not after ten years of missing him in her life.

They met near the hospital's main entrance, had a friendly word with security man Donald Orr, and then made their way back to her flat. The morning drizzle had ceased and it was now cool but bright. As they arrived and went indoors, the silence between them grew ever more tense. Perhaps Luke had changed his mind. After all, he'd not mentioned it again all week.

Nervous and edgy, she turned to face him and saw the same feelings reflected in his sultry green eyes. Strangely, his own air of uncertainty made her feel better.

'I need your answer. What are you going to do, Chessie?' Luke's husky voice finally broke the silence that had stretched between them, asking the question that had weighed on both their minds all week. 'Are you going to stay here alone, or will you come back with me for the weekend?'

When it came right down to it, after days of endless worry and indecision, her choice was an easy one, temptation being impossible to resist. 'I'll come with you,' she agreed, barely above a whisper.

But clearly Luke had heard, as relief and needy desire flared in his eyes. 'Thank you.'

'I'll, um, just put some things in a bag.' Now the decision had been made, her heart was thudding wildly against her ribs and she had no idea what to do. Hesitating, she turned to face him. 'What do I bring?'

'Yourself. A toothbrush.' He smiled, more relaxed now.

'I meant clothes and things.'

His eyes glittered like green fire, scorching

her. 'Whatever makes you comfortable. I doubt we'll we wearing much.'

Heat flared through her from her breasts to her womb, pooling in a heavy throb between her thighs. She knew what she was agreeing to by going with him. There was excitement. But she was also scared. Scared it meant so much more to her than to him, scared that however hot, however blissfully decadent this weekend, it would never be enough. Scared that walking away on Monday was going to be the hardest thing she had ever done.

Filled with doubts and myriad emotions, she returned to the living room with the few things she had packed, finding Luke standing where she had left him. Waiting. He held out his hand, asking a silent question, and she answered by placing her own hand in his, sealing her delicious—but dangerous—fate.

Once in the car, the first part of the journey passed in a blur for Francesca, the silence growing again. She glanced at Luke's profile and realised that he seemed tense, nervous, and she wondered why. And then she focused on where they were. Strathlochan had been growing in recent years but you only needed to go a short way outside the town to be in beautiful, secluded countryside. Francesca found her hands clenching on the sides of the passenger seat as Luke guided the car down a narrow, hedge-lined road between rolling fields and pockets of native woodland, the hills rising high in the near distance. A familiar road. A road she remembered from her teens but had not visited for years—except in her dreams.

When Luke slowed and turned the car off the road onto a short gravel standing beside a pretty, slate-roofed, stone-built cottage and switched off the engine, Francesca thought she must be dreaming again. She could feel each beat of her pulse in her throat, every rapid breath that huffed in and out of her lungs, her disbelieving gaze taking in every long-remembered, lichen-spotted stone and slate of this building with the sprawling tangle of honeysuckle rambling up one side, the high mixed beech and hawthorn hedge that hid the garden. She had once climbed a tree on a school nature walk to peer into that garden.

For this was *her* cottage. *Her* dream home. This was the place she had kept as an ideal image in her mind as she had worked hard to achieve her goals. A place she had regularly passed on boring training runs, a place that had lived in her fantasies, giving her something to aim for. A place that had been central in her imaginary world, the one that was so much better than her reality.

Tears threatened as she turned to face Luke. He sat quietly, watching her, nervousness, hope, doubt, excitement and so much more all reflected in his eyes. Somehow she found her voice, hoarse and wobbly though it sounded.

'You live here?'

'Yes.'

The single word hovered between them and Francesca wrestled with her thoughts, trying to remember all he had told her. 'You bought this place nearly five years ago?'

This time he nodded in confirmation, remaining silent. He'd bought this cottage after his father had died, she recalled, when his mother had returned from London to live in Strathlochan. It had been an investment, he'd told her. Long after she had left town, longer still since they had seen each other. So was it just a coincidence? Could he have known? And if he had, why would he buy it when he never expected to live in it or see her again?

'Why?' So many questions pounded through her mind, but that was the only one she could voice.

'When I was helping Ma find her town house, I saw the particulars for this place in the Solicitors' Property Centre.' He looked away, gazing at the house for several moments before turning back to her, green eyes serious, genuine emotion in his husky voice. 'I'd searched for you but you'd gone. And I saw the cottage and remembered it had been your dream. It became my dream, too…something of you I could hold on to. So I bought it. And I never gave up hope that one day I could bring you here.'

The tears that had shimmered on her lashes spilled onto her cheeks. 'I can't believe you did this,' she whispered, unable to make sense of all the meanings and implications and ramifications of what he had done and why.

But right at that moment, as his fingers gently brushed the moisture from her cheeks, the whys and wherefores and the seriousness of the future didn't matter. Luke had done this—for her. Never knowing whether or not they might meet again, he'd had a dream too, and he'd done it.

'Did I do wrong?'

The anxiety behind his words permeated the

fog in her brain and she shook her head, laughing and crying at the same time. Fumbling with the handle, she opened the door and slid out, waiting for Luke to join her. Taking his hand, she gave him a tremulous, teary smile.

'I want to see *everything*,' she told him. 'I've never been inside before, but can we go in through the garden and see if it's the same as I remember?'

Linking his fingers with hers, Luke led her down the path beside the house to a high, narrow wooden gate. Her heart was in her mouth. No one had ever done anything like this for her before. No one had ever thought of her, wanted something special for her. It was almost too much to take in. And, if it were possible, it was even more glorious than her dreams because now—even if only for this weekend—she could pretend it was all real.

CHAPTER EIGHT

LUKE couldn't help smiling at Francesca's almost childlike enjoyment. They'd explored the garden, which she'd told him was much bigger than she remembered from her brief glimpse through the tree branches well over a decade ago. The small orchard was the still there but there was more space, hidden corners and a whole area around the other side of the building where the flower borders were less groomed and looked to be packed with rambling cottage garden plants and wildflowers which would provide a riot of colour in the weeks and months ahead.

'It's even better than I'd imagined it,' she admitted once they moved indoors. 'And so much bigger than you'd think from outside.'

He hung back, allowing her to roam through the surprisingly large kitchen with its original stone-flagged floor, the range which radiated comforting warmth, the custom-built wooden units with granite work surfaces and the large butler's sink by the window that overlooked the garden. He had kept the farmhouse table that bore the marks of several generations who had lived in this house...like so much else, it felt as if it belonged.

As Francesca moved along the passageway to the cosy living room, Luke tried to see it through her eyes, wondering how she was feeling and if the place lived up to her expectations. He knew she was surprised to discover he owned the cottage and he'd both enjoyed her shock but been terrified by it, unsure if she would be pleased or if it would have ruined everything.

'It's a bit untidy,' he apologised, self-consciously clearing things up.

'Don't worry, I like it.' Her reassurance sounded genuine, so he stopped bothering. About that, at least. 'It's lived in. Warm. Homely. The complete opposite of where I grew up.'

As she paused, moving around, a faint smile on her face as she trailed her fingertips along the ancient beam that served as mantlepiece above the fireplace, Luke recalled the posh-looking house in the expensive part of town where she had lived with her mother. The antithesis of his family's circumstances. Outwardly, it had seemed Francesca had had everything money could buy, but he'd known better…that she had always lacked the priceless thing she had needed most—love.

'My mother was obsessed with appearances and with everything being in its place,' she continued, almost as if talking to herself. 'My own bedroom had to be just so, tidied to military precision. I was scared to sit down in case I displaced a cushion.' She laughed but it held the pain of the past as she revealed more about how rigid and unloved her young life had been. 'It was a house. *This* is a home.'

But could it be the home Francesca would share with him for ever or would the gloss of this excitement wear off once the realities of everything hit her? Well aware of the dangers that still lay ahead, he left her alone to wander and returned to the kitchen to put together the supper he had prepared in the hope she would come back with him that evening. How could he convince Francesca that dreams *could* be real, that for them this *could* work? One step at a time, he told himself. Make the weekend special.

And if she walked away on Monday, if she needed time, he had to give her some space, however painful and difficult it was going to be for him. He had to believe that nothing this right and good would ultimately fail, that eventually Francesca would see what they had and come to believe, too. Hope was all he had to hold on to.

He called her when the meal was ready—fresh Scottish salmon, new potatoes and broccoli, things he knew Francesca loved—but, delicious as it was, neither of them seemed hungry. At least, not for food. Luke certainly wasn't. But aware of the electric tension and build-up of sexual energy, he was trying to keep things as normal as possible for Francesca, whose nervousness was evident.

The small-talk was uncharacteristically stilted. Wanting her to relax, he made them each some hot chocolate and carried the mugs through to the sitting room. While the April days were getting warmer, the nights were still chilly and Luke lit the fire he had set, waiting for the kindling to catch and settle before adding some seasoned, fragrant logs. He sat back on his heels and looked at Chessie, who was perched on the edge of the sofa, her mug cupped in her hands.

She had the most incredible hair he had ever seen. The colour was extraordinary and difficult to describe—a vibrant mix of all the colours of autumn. In the gentle light of the room and with the glow of the fire flickering, it was silken, shining and framed her face like a halo of russet flame. Long and lustrous, it hung loose to the small of her back in bouncy corkscrew curls, with burnished copper tendrils feathering around her face and neck. Luke wanted to feel her hair against his skin, wanted to see it fanned out across his pillow, wanted to sink his hands into the thick vibrancy of it when she was beneath him, breathless with passion, and his body was sinking into hers again and again.

But that was for later. First he needed to deal with her anxiety. Still on his knees, he edged closer to her and set his empty mug on the low table. When she put her own mug aside, he took her hand in his, feeling the customary jolt of current at the connection of her skin against his. He could also feel the faint tremble of her fingers. Drawing them to his lips, he brushed a feather-light caress across her palm, looking up to meet silver-grey eyes that reflected the flickering firelight but also a whole jumble of raw emotions.

'You're nervous about this.'

Francesca nodded, feeling foolish, unable to look away from the slow-burn desire in Luke's smoky green eyes. His touch both distracted and aroused her. As did his closeness. Not to mention the beguiling knowledge of where she was. The house was better than any dream she had ever had of it, so much more in reality than she had imagined. And so was Luke. She wanted him… but she was scared.

'Has someone hurt you in the past, Chessie?'

'No, nothing like that. It's just…' She clammed up, unable to go on.

'What?' he cajoled, his fingers playing with hers. 'Tell me. It's important.'

Doubt and embarrassment overwhelmed her. 'The couple of times I've done it before I've not enjoyed it,' she finally admitted.

As Luke shifted even closer, her thighs instinctively parted so he was kneeling between them, his hands sliding up her arms to her shoulders, drawing her into a hug.

'Nothing is going to happen that you don't

want, Chessie,' he reassured her, voice low and husky. 'Tell me what happened before that's making you so tense and jumpy, what they did that you didn't like.'

She felt shy talking like this with him, not wanting him to feel less of her for the mistakes she had made. But she also felt safe in Luke's arms and the shadowed light in the room inspired the sharing of confidences.

'You can always tell me anything.' As ever, he seemed to know just what to say, and now, as if reading her hesitancy, his words and tone gave her comfort. 'If I know what went wrong, I can make sure I don't do something to upset you.'

'It's not you.'

He waited patiently for her to speak, the soothing caress of his hands and the warmth of him being close helped set her at ease and she found herself telling him about Edinburgh.

'I've never wanted a relationship, I've always believed I was better alone. Yet twice over those years while I was training I ended up having a one-night stand. Ever since I've felt ashamed I ever did it.'

'Don't do that to yourself, Chessie,' he chided gently, one hand stroking her hair, his fingers

216 THE REBEL SURGEON'S PROPOSAL

sinking into her curls to gently massage the back of her neck. 'I can assure you that you are not the only person who has been lonely and sought physical comfort. I've been there, too, and I did the same as you in the past.'

'It doesn't bring what you need,' she whispered, her head resting on his shoulder, her eyes closing as she breathed in the familiar scent of him.

'No, it doesn't.'

Soothed by his voice, his understanding, his caressing touch, she leaned more into him. 'Aside from being inexperienced, I found it intimidating. It was all about what they wanted, and I couldn't let go or participate because I didn't feel anything.'

'Chessie, I know better than anyone how you need to feel secure and in control.' Luke drew back a little, cupping her face in his hands, his green eyes filled with sincerity and heart-stopping desire.

'But how do you know it will be any different? How do you know I won't disappoint you?' she finally asked, voicing two of her greatest anxieties.

Warm breath brushed her skin as he chuckled softly. 'Chessie, I can assure you that you will not disappoint me and I know it will be different for both of us because of how we already feel.' One hand fisted in her hair, tilting her head so he could look at her, forcing her to look at him. 'I have *never* felt with anyone else the way I do when I look at you, touch you, kiss you. That's how I know. It is you and me and it's right.'

His answer increased her wariness because she knew it was true. Which made it all the more serious and sounding less like the fun weekend she had pretended to herself that was all this was going to be. Before she could wrestle with her thoughts and her doubts, Luke continued, the fingers of his free hand whispering over her face, the pad of his thumb tracing the fullness of her lower lip.

'It's about give and take, Chessie. Mutual pleasure. And about trust. If I do anything you don't like or want, then you say so and I stop. For me it's as much if not more about your pleasure than my own. Because yours makes mine. It's about trusting each other. And because we do, we can let go and be safe. We can just take our time and see where it leads us. OK?'

Francesca sucked in a shaky breath. His kindness and understanding made her want to cry, yet for all her belief that she didn't enjoy sex, just being near Luke fired her blood and every touch, every look, every kiss made her want as she had never wanted before. Just as he had said. She had no idea what happened after this night, this weekend. She didn't want to think that far ahead because, despite Luke's reassurances to the contrary, she was still scared it might ruin the friendship between them. But she had come too far to turn back. The inescapable truth she could no longer deny to herself was that she wanted to know what it was like to make love with Luke.

'OK,' she whispered.

She heard him release a shaky breath of relief, but the heat in his eyes as they looked deeply into hers seared through her body and left her in no doubt about his feelings, his desire, his need of her. As his lips brushed across hers, gentle, testing, teasing, but already causing a storm to rage inside her, her blood started careening through her veins.

Her mouth opened of its own volition, inviting, demanding the full onslaught of the mutual explosion of passion between them. She clung to him, revelling in his taste, welcoming the deepening of the kiss, her own tongue instinctively duelling and mating with his invading one. A whimper of regret escaped when Luke pulled back, leaving her bereft and wanting more, but the protest she was about to voice died when he slowly drew his jumper, and the T-shirt beneath, over his head and tossed them aside.

Francesca wasn't sure she could breathe as she absorbed the first sight of Luke stripped to the waist, all that rippling muscle and golden skin reflected in the glow of the firelight. Her own temperature rose several degrees, just looking at all that masculine perfection. She wanted to touch, to taste, shocked at the strength of her hungry need. It was so unlike her. But everything about Luke was different, made her different, called to something unknown deep within her.

His gaze never left hers as he took one of her hands and drew it to him, holding her palm flat to his chest right over his heart. She could feel his heat, feel the texture of his skin, feel the racing of his pulse. A narrow line of darker blond hair arrowed down from his chest, centred his toned stomach and ducked under the waistband of his jeans. Trailing one finger downwards, she enjoyed the way he sucked in a shaky breath, seeing and feeling the reaction as his muscles tensed.

Being with Luke gave her the freedom to relax and explore. She leaned forward and set her mouth to his skin, tasting the male flavour of him, earthy, slightly salty, delicious. He groaned as her lips and tongue followed the path of her finger. Arms wrapping around her, he drew her with him as he lay back on the soft rug in front of the fire. On top she felt in control and made the most of the opportunity he had given to her.

But all too soon it wasn't enough. She wanted—needed—for him to touch *her*. Surprising herself, she sat up, straddling his thighs and slowly unbuttoned her top, her heart pounding, each breath rasping in her lungs, excited by the hungry look in Luke's darkening green eyes as he watched her undress for him. She certainly felt the reaction in the hard demand of his body under hers. With a confidence she hadn't known she possessed, she tossed the top aside and then unhooked the fastening of her bra, nervousness returning as she slid the straps down her arms and exposed herself to him for the first time.

'You're beautiful, Chessie.' His voice was raw,

throaty, and sent tingles of awareness and arousal down her spine. 'Perfect. I want to touch you and kiss you all over.'

Wanting that too, appreciating that he left her in control, she took his hands and, copying his actions earlier, she slowly brought them towards her until his palms covered her breasts. She was unable to withhold her soft cry at the first feel of his touch on her sensitive, hardened nipples. Arching her back as he shaped and caressed her, she clung to him, giving herself up to the unexpected and searing pleasure that rolled like waves through her body.

'Luke…'

He sat up and she locked her arms around him, melting into his kiss, her torso pressed to his, overwhelmed by sensations she had never experienced before. The urgency grew until she could bear it no longer, then nerveless fingers were wrestling with the fastening of his jeans. Luke moved to help her, far more expert in disposing of her remaining clothes, rolling her to the side to give each of them easier access to explore and discover but without her feeling intimidated or held down.

Francesca lost focus as she gave herself up to

Luke's passionate seduction. His hands and his mouth left no part of her untouched. She felt cherished, desired. And emboldened by his husky words of encouragement, her hands enjoyed an exploration of their own, learning the planes and contours and textures of his muscled body. Her fingers reached his erection and instinctively wrapped around him, cautious at first, discovering what he enjoyed, revelling in his responses, his groan of pleasure. Imagining how he was going to feel inside her, impatience increased.

But Luke kept her waiting, indulging himself in learning her body, teasing her as he took his time pretending to count the freckles across her collarbones. She gasped, her hold on him tightening as his lips, teeth and tongue worked down to her breasts, drawing each nipple in turn into the moist heat of his mouth, tormenting, suckling deeply, bringing her to fever pitch. And when she didn't think she could bear any more, his mouth journeyed on, pausing at her navel, which she had never known was so sensitive, before sliding lower still, leaving her breathless and boneless with pleasure as he settled between her thighs.

Francesca's fingers clenched in the thickness

of Luke's hair, crying out at the delicious shock as his mouth and fingers took her higher and higher. Control was slipping away from her and she didn't care. She couldn't think of anything but the incredible pleasure as Luke took her over the edge into oblivion.

As she slowly regained her senses, Luke was reaching for his discarded jeans and rummaging in the pocket for a condom. He rolled onto his back, taking her with him, handing the packet to her. Still shaking from the force of her orgasm, her heart racing, she opened the foil with trembling fingers, hesitating, taking her time as she slowly rolled it on.

'Chessie, sweetheart.' Luke's voice was hoarse, his whole body rigid with tension. 'You're killing me…please. I need you. Now.'

Her moment of awkwardness was stripped away by the urgency of his need and the answering ache of her own body. He gave her control, guiding her as she slid over him. Slowly, oh, so slowly, she sank down, closing her eyes as she savoured the exquisite sensations of being filled so completely, so wonderfully by Luke. Her gasp of shocked delight mingled with his groan and she forced open her eyes, staring down at him, seeing his own darkened with hungry passion. For her.

'Move,' he begged her, his hands sliding up her thighs to span her hips.

Unable to keep still another second, she did as he bade, the flickering glow from the fire casting shadows over the age-old dance of their bodies. Her hair cascaded wildly around her as she set the rhythm. One of Luke's hands fisted in it, drawing her down to take her mouth in a blistering kiss. She met and matched him, striving for the ultimate resolution. But even that was not enough. She had control but found she no longer wanted it. She needed more. Needed everything, Needed all of Luke.

'What's wrong?' Luke asked, as if sensing a change in her as she hesitated.

She shook her head, lying on top of him, a shiver of delicious sensation rippling through her as her sensitive breasts grazed his chest. Adjusting her hold, she encouraged him to roll over.

His free hand cupped her face. 'You're sure, Chessie?'

'Yes.'

Excitement coursed through her at the smouldering expression in his eyes as he reversed their positions and his weight came down on top of her. Instinctively her body arched up to him. With one hand locked in her hair, Luke slid his other arm under her hips, holding her to him as he entered her with a deep, heavy thrust. Francesca sobbed, writhing beneath him, wrapping her legs around him, crying out as he set his own rhythm.

'More,' she pleaded in a heated whisper, clinging to him, needing to feel all of him everywhere, afraid they would combust with the heat of the flames that raged between them.

'You're mine, Chessie.' Luke said the words again and again as they came together, but she barely registered them, too lost was she in the raging inferno of their passion. 'Mine.'

When she thought she had reached the height of bliss, Luke took her even further, then further still, before falling with her into an endless abyss of unimagined pleasure. Crying his name, she held on to him, uncaring if she never surfaced again, because nothing on earth could be as special and amazing as what they had just shared. They collapsed together, spent and drained, in front of the dying embers of the fire.

She could hear Luke's breathing as ragged as her own and feel the frenetic beat of his heart in time with hers. She had thought sex dull, unmoving, a waste of time? How wrong she had been. How right and wonderful it was… with Luke.

Francesca had no idea how much time had passed before Luke moved, then she was aware of him lifting her in his arms and carrying her sleepy form through to the bathroom. After tying her hair up to keep it out of the water, he snapped on the shower and together they stepped under the spray. She leaned into him as he took the soap and lathered her body, lingering over her breasts, her nipples hardening impossibly again, her whole being buzzing as he washed her intimately. She returned the favour, lazily gliding soapy hands over his body.

'No birthmarks,' she murmured, feeling as well as hearing his throaty chuckle.

'And I still have lots of lovely freckles to count and explore.'

He laughed again as she groaned, but her groan turned to a gasp as he knelt down and, hooking one of her knees over his shoulder, set his mouth to the feminine heart of her and rocked her world all over again. Francesca whimpered and sank against him, too shaky to stand unaided. His hands cupped her rear, shaping gently, holding her steady, and she gripped his shoulders, not sure how much more she could take of the erotic assault on her senses.

Francesca lost all sense of time. The next thing she was aware of was Luke towelling them both dry, and then he was tucking her into his bed and snuggling up with her. She rested her head against him, feeling sheltered and protected with his arms around her. Not to mention deliciously exhausted. She'd never spent the whole night in bed with a man before and was surprised she wasn't more unsettled.

They talked softly for a while…about the house, old memories, Luke's mother. Francesca had no idea what made her ask her next question but the words were out before she could stop them.

'Have you never been in love?'

'Only once in my life, Chessie.'

Luke's voice was heavy with sleep but his reply brought a searing swell of jealousy that threatened to rip her to shreds. She stiffened, wondering who the woman was, raising her head to look at him in the dim light.

'Do you still love her?' she persisted, angry with herself.

Luke's eyes were closed but a smile touched his mouth. 'I'll love her for ever.'

She froze in shocked despair at the softness of his voice. 'So why aren't you with her?'

'At the moment she doesn't feel the same way I do.'

Francesca frowned at the admission, hating the sadness he'd been unable to hide. The woman, whoever she was, had to be crazy to let Luke get away, to throw his love back at him. Fighting the sudden welling of tears, she set her head down on his chest again, feeling and hearing his steady heartbeat.

'I hope it works out for you,' she managed, a catch in her voice.

His hand stroked her hair and he drew her closer. 'So do I, sweetheart.'

Luke slipped into sleep a long while before she did. She'd had the most amazing night of her life, experienced things she had only read about in books and had never believed she could feel in real life. And then she had ruined it all by asking Luke those questions and learning of his love for another woman. She had never wanted to be loved by a man, had never wanted a relationship or closeness, had asked no more than friendship from Luke, so why did she now feel so wretched?

For Luke the weekend flew by far too quickly. They woke very late on Saturday morning. The post had brought a note for him and Francesca from Conor and Kate Anderson, along with a squiggly 'Thank you' from Rebecca for her birthday present. Also enclosed was a photo of Rebecca cuddled up with her huge toy elephant, which made both him and Francesca laugh. And Luke thought again how he longed for a gaggle of mini-Chessies of his own, just as Conor had Kate and Rebecca.

Aside from her enjoyment of the note and photo, Francesca seemed quiet and he vaguely remembered a whispered conversation before they had fallen asleep, something about never being in love. He hoped to goodness he hadn't frightened her off by confessing the true extent of his feelings for her. So he didn't refer to it. Instead, he began a detailed exploration to count the freckles sprinkled across the back of her shoulders...or intended to, until he was distracted and made love to her again, showing her with his body everything he could not yet tell her in words.

As he had suspected, under that ice maiden reserve, a façade he understood all too well, Francesca was a sensual, feisty woman, a side of her he longed to bring out and explore and keep all to himself. In just a few hours she had blossomed, responding to him instinctively, sharing a depth and extent of passion and pleasure he'd never known before. He could only hope this weekend would win her over— or at least give her something to think about so she wouldn't reject him completely.

In the afternoon they went to the animal shelter and, after a few chores, enjoyed another walk with Murphy and Harry. The only downside came when Sally Hislop, the spirited and inde-fatigable owner of the centre, told Francesca that, after months of waiting, a perfect new owner had been found for the two huge and lovable Newfoundlands.

'I can't believe I won't be seeing or walking them again,' Francesca murmured as they arrived back at his cottage. 'I'm glad they'll have a good home, but…'

Her sentence trailed off and Luke drew her forlorn figure into his arms, not having the words at that moment to comfort her. So he distracted her the best way he could and took her to bed.

Which was pretty much where they stayed all day on Sunday. It helped that it rained, keeping them indoors. And, really, there was nowhere else he wanted to be but with her. So they spent hours making love, sleeping, talking and making love again.

It was amazing.

Francesca was amazing.

And then it was Monday afternoon and time to take her home. Luke wanted to rage and protest, to kidnap her until she understood and recognised what he had known all along…that they were meant to be together, two halves of a whole. But on the drive back into town, Francesca again grew silent and Luke felt sick with nerves. She'd said she wanted a bit of time at her flat alone to get ready for the first of their three upcoming night shifts, but with each minute he felt her slipping away from him again. He drew up outside her flat and switched off the engine, at a loss to know how to get through to her.

'Thank you for this weekend, Luke.' Her gaze

flicked towards him and away again, her fingers nervously toying with the strap of her bag. 'I had a good time.'

The words and their polite delivery, as if all that had passed between them had been some bland and pleasant outing rather than the blaze of passion, broke through his calm control. Despite knowing he should handle Francesca with patience, all his feelings came pouring out in an unstoppable tide.

'A good time? Is that all this was to you? This wasn't just a weekend that meant nothing. Not for me. I understand your fears and I know you need time. But this weekend was a taste of what the rest of our lives could be like, Chessie.'

Francesca stared at Luke, shocked by his vehemence and also by his words. 'What do you mean?'

'You're mine, Francesca, you always have been. As I am yours.' His hand snaked out, his fingers fisting in her hair, preventing her looking away from the fiercely determined expression in his green eyes. 'It's taken ten years to find you again, and now that I have, I'm not letting you go. You're the only woman I've ever loved, ever needed, the only person aside from Ma who has ever cared about me, believed in me, respected me. And you feel nothing at all?'

'I do care about you, I do feel the attraction, but I don't know I have it in me to commit. I've always been alone, Luke. You know that. The one person I should have been able to depend on and trust, my mother, let me down, lied to me, used me, betrayed me.'

'And you think I did the same when I left town,' he said, his voice hollow and with an edge of bitter regret.

Unshed tears spiked her lashes as she fought her confused emotions. 'Not knowingly, not like that. But it made me stronger alone. It made me believe I could never depend on anyone but myself. How do I know you won't go again? How do you know what we have will last?'

'All I know is that I love you, that being with you makes me stronger, more complete, and happier than I've ever been. I didn't leave you— I left Strathlochan because I had no choice. And as soon as I could, I came back. For you. But you were gone and I couldn't find you. Yet I never forgot and never gave up hope.' He paused, his hand still locked in her hair. 'When Ma broke her arm and told me you were here, all I could think about was coming back for you. It took me eight weeks to organise everything—to pack up, to leave the professor's team, to get the job here. It was the longest eight weeks I've known because I was so desperate to see you again, to know if it was still there.

'And it was, Chessie,' he continued, filled with the passion she had come to know. 'The second I saw you in that corridor, I knew the connection had never been broken, that ten years apart had changed nothing, had only made you more beautiful and special, and my love for you even stronger and deeper. I need you, Chessie. You are the other part of me that makes me whole. I came back to Strathlochan for three reasons…for Ma and for the job, yes… But the most important reason of all was coming back here for *you*. You hold my heart in your hands. I'll never leave you, I'll always love you, I'll always be here for you, whatever you want or need. You have to decide what that is and if it's enough for you.'

Francesca was speechless with shock. *She* was the main reason he'd come back to Strathlochan? He loved her? It was *her* he had talked about in the night, the one woman he wished could love him back? It was all too much to take in at once.

'It's always been you, Chessie. And always will be. We were destined to be together,' he insisted.

'No one is ever going to control me again.'

He cursed in frustration, giving her a gentle shake. 'It's not about domination or control. It's opening yourself up that sets you free, Chessie. Do you think I'm not vulnerable to you? I am. You have all the power here. I'm totally exposed to you. My heart, my happiness, my life, they are in your hands. I trust you because I love you. We're equals, Chessie, partners, sharing the gift, so much stronger together as a unit than we could ever be alone.'

'Luke…' She couldn't doubt the passionate sincerity of his words but she was scared. Scared and confused.

'I need you to need me as much as I need you. It's a partnership of equals, Chessie. We work because we love each other, desire each other, but you're still fighting it, still so desperate not to give an inch of control. I don't want to use it against you but to give it back and so much more. To know you trust me as much as I trust you.'

He released her, pushing open his door and getting out. She watched, her heart thudding, her mind racing, as he walked round the car and held the passenger door open for her. Legs shaking, she climbed out, her hands clutching her bag in a death grip. Taking her by surprise, Luke cupped her face with gentle hands and kissed her, hot, hard and passionate, before he stepped back. Green eyes, turbulent with emotion, looked at her for a long moment.

'I may freely give you everything I have in me and of me, Chessie, but I need at least something back from you,' he told her, voice husky and laced with sadness and a thread of defeat. 'If and when you can do that, if you want my love and all we can have together, let me know.'

Francesca stared after him as he drove away. She had never wanted to hurt Luke, but the shadows of pain in his eyes had shown her that she had. He'd laid everything open for her. This strong, independent man had made himself vulnerable for her, had given her everything, every part of him, and she had let him walk away.

Could she commit? Did she deserve Luke's love? Could *she* love him back as he deserved to be loved? She had so much to think about.

But, basically, what it came down to was a simple choice. Life with Luke or life without Luke.

What was she going to do?

CHAPTER NINE

'THE first priority is to get this haemorrhaging under control or we are going to lose her.'

A and E consultant Robert Mowbray's words greeted Luke as he hurried into the resus bay in the early hours of Tuesday morning in response to the urgent page he had received. The medical team was hard at work, caring for the stricken patient, and, he noted, Francesca was already present, taking X-rays.

'C-spine, please, Francesca,' Robert requested. 'But I want to concentrate on pelvic images before we worry about anything else.'

Even in such a tense situation, just seeing Francesca stirred Luke's blood, made his heart beat faster and brought a welter of thoughts and emotions—

'Luke, you're here. Just the man. We need your expertise.'

'What do we have?' Luke asked, snapping back into his professional role when Robert had finished issuing instructions to his staff and turned to greet him.

'This is Diane, aged fifty-two. She'd been out at a party where there had been a fair bit of drinking and merriment. As it was breaking up, she slipped over in the car park and a vehicle reversed over her hips and pelvis—one wheel. The driver never saw her,' Robert explained, giving details of Diane's overall condition since. 'The initial suggestion is of an open-book fracture of the pelvis but Francesca is doing some detailed X-rays.'

Luke looked at the monitors displaying Diane's vital signs, concerned at the deterioration evident there. 'Internal bleeding?'

'That's my fear. Diane was conscious on arrival but is fading in and out now. The anaesthetist is on the way down. We've sent blood for urgent cross-matching.'

'Any other fractures?' Luke asked, looking over the notes and examining the area of injury.

'None suspected on first review,' Robert responded. 'Her rib cage is clear, femurs feel intact, but we'll do a thorough secondary assessment once we've stemmed this pelvic bleed. We've used a splint wrap, hoping it would compress the pelvis and halt the blood loss,' the consultant continued, his concern and frustration evident, 'but despite that, and the fluid replacement, nothing we are doing is improving things and her BP continues to drop. She needs surgery now.'

'And all the theatres are in use thanks to the motorway collision earlier tonight.' Luke delivered the bad news, unsurprised when the consultant cursed in annoyance. He had an idea but he'd need to make arrangements with his boss before proceeding. 'Maurice is operating but I'll ask him to spare some help so I can do a temporary fixation here in Resus.'

Robert indicated his understanding and agreement. 'Not easy, and not ideal conditions in terms of cleanliness outside an operating room, but unless we do something, Diane won't last much longer, bleeding out as she is. If you can do it, Luke, you'll buy her time and save her life.'

'Let's hope so.'

'Tell me what you need. We'll give you all the support we can.'

Grateful for the older man's faith in him, Luke smiled. 'Thanks.'

'While you look at the X-rays and gather together your equipment, I'll send a nurse to the blood bank to chase up the units we need and ask for some more. And I'll update Diane's family. I think the shock has rapidly sobered up her poor husband,' Robert informed him, shaking his head as he moved away.

Luke waited for Francesca to finish, admiring the way she went about her work with calm efficiency. There had been some awkwardness when they had met up at the hospital after the way they had parted at her flat hours earlier, but they'd both been professional. Whilst he was sorry that anyone had been injured, the fact that the night shift had been so busy had helped them both to focus on the job and had given him less time to brood. And to worry if he'd made the biggest mistake of his life by losing his patience and rushing her.

He'd done everything he could, had laid his heart on the line, had bared his soul, and now all he could do was wait and see whether it was enough, whether his love could ever compensate for the pain and loneliness and loss that had been all Francesca had known for so long. He didn't blame her for her lack of trust. He *had* left. At eighteen he hadn't understood how that would hurt her and he had never intended to be away so long. At sixteen, she would never have understood why or have known he was coming back. It had been just one more in a long line of betrayals. Could she get past that? They needed each other. Would she see that, or would she reject all he was offering her?

It was proving harder than he had ever imagined to act normally and to hide his hurt and his fear. He knew she needed time, but she gave no clues about what she was thinking or feeling. He had no one to blame but himself if he'd ruined everything by declaring himself and demanding her surrender before she was ready to contemplate it.

'The pictures are ready.' Francesca's words drew him back from his thoughts.

'Thanks.' Stepping closer to examine the screen also allowed him to enjoy her subtle flowery scent, enough that he was blinded for a moment by the memories of their weekend together, the feel and taste of her. On dangerous ground, he snapped himself back into work mode. 'Let's see what we have.'

'It looks like a classic open-book fracture, as Robert suspected.'

Sure enough, the pelvis had snapped and opened out. Like a polo mint, the rigid ring of the pelvis never broke in just one place. Luke flicked to another image, planning what was necessary and seeing the shadows of fluid in the cavity, which indicated the evidence of the pooling of blood Diane was losing internally.

'What are you going to do?' Francesca asked, her interest evident.

'With the theatres unavailable, I'm going to have to do a procedure here in Resus. I'll put screws in and externally fixate the pelvis in place,' he explained, drawing her a hasty diagram. 'The plan is to hold the pelvis in position and stop the bleeding so that we can stabilise Diane. That will buy us some time for a permanent repair and also to investigate any other injuries, including assessment of possible complications…for example, her urinary situation in case of damage to her bladder.'

Word came down from Maurice instructing Luke, as Specialist Registrar, to carry out the procedure. Moments later a couple of the more junior orthopaedic team doctors arrived in Resus to assist, closely followed by matronly A and E nurse Gail, returning somewhat breathlessly from the blood bank with several cross-matched units of blood.

'Blood pressure still falling,' one of the medical team called out as Robert returned from talking to Diane's family.

'Right,' Luke said after scrubbing up, hiding any flicker of nervousness. 'We're set to go.'

With the anaesthetist happy with Diane's condition, and the blood transfusion being pushed through at full volume, Luke prepared to begin, well aware of the responsibility resting on his shoulders to get this right. Working in the Resus bay was very different from the sterile, fully equipped operating theatre he was used to. It was also more cramped. Knowing that Francesca was nearby, looking on, he glanced up and met her gaze. Her tiny smile of encouragement, signalling her confidence in him, brought an inner calmness as he bent to his task.

Diane's skin had been swabbed with antiseptic to disinfect the area and, using the detailed X-ray images Francesca had already taken to guide his positioning, Luke set about making the first of the four small incisions necessary. With each one he cut carefully down through the layers of tissue and muscle to locate the pelvic bones and then prepared to insert the screws. One of the assisting team worked to suction out the blood. When each screw was in place, four rods protruded from Diane's body to which an external frame was attached, pulling the pelvis back together to keep it rigid and supported.

'Can we have another X-ray please, Francesca?' Luke asked, straightening and mentally running over all he had done to ensure there had been no mistakes. 'I want to check that everything is positioned properly.'

Those not wearing protective lead aprons stepped out of the way as Francesca manoeuvred the imaging machine into place and took the required pictures. Watching the screen, Luke breathed a sigh of relief when it became apparent that the screws *were* correctly positioned and that the external fixator cradle was already doing its job.

'Her blood pressure is rising and she's stabilising!'

The announcement brought a collective sigh of relief, which continued to grow as Diane's vital signs improved after the emergency operation, the seven units of cross-matched blood and nearly two litres of fluid replacing the blood that had haemorrhaged to fill the pelvic cavity.

'Thanks, everyone, I appreciate your help,' Luke praised, grateful for the help both of the A and E team and his own orthopaedic colleagues. 'We've closed the ring, stopped things moving around and controlled the bleeding. Now we need to send Diane for a CT scan so we can assess the extent of her pelvic injuries and ensure there are no chest, abdominal or hip problems.'

A hand landed on his shoulder. 'An impressive job, Luke. Well done,' Robert congratulated him.

'Thank you, sir.' The older consultant's opinion meant a lot to him. 'We still have a long way to go with Diane.'

'Indeed. Let's get her through to Radiology so we can take a detailed CT scan. You carry on.'

Robert's approval and tacit invitation to maintain control of Diane's care for this stage of the process bolstered Luke's confidence. Checking that the patient's condition was stable, Luke gathered the small team together and followed as the trolley bed was wheeled through to the radiology department and into the CT scan room for the next step in Diane's care.

For the moment, at least, thoughts of Francesca, and her decision on whether she would accept or reject him were going to have to wait.

Luke was in Theatre, completing the repair of an elbow fracture to a motorcyclist, when their shift officially ended on Tuesday morning. Francesca had no idea how long he might be but she felt an overwhelming need to see him. She had experienced a rush of pride at his achievements during the early hours with Diane in Resus. His skill had been obvious, the procedure an important one, but he'd worked calmly and shown no sign that the tense atmosphere around the patient had affected him.

She had accompanied the small group that had gone with Diane for the CT scan. The three-hundred-and-sixty-degree orientation showed slices through the body and the computer as-similated the information and displayed the pictures as 3-D images. Everyone had been relieved that Diane's injuries were confined to the pelvis, but she was not out of the woods yet. Luke's temporary repair had saved Diane's life, but complications remained—there were concerns about her bladder and it was likely she would need further surgery.

It had been a hectic night shift and Francesca had been glad of work to keep her busy, but it had not stopped her mind from working overtime about Luke. There had been a new awkwardness between them during their working hours, as hard as they had both tried to act normally. And while part of her longed for things to be back the way they had been before, she had not been able to stop thinking about their weekend together—or to regret it.

Even now her body throbbed with need and she was deliciously tender from the extent of their enjoyment of each other. She had never been desired as Luke desired her. It had been a little alarming at first but soon she had felt a sense of power that his need for her made him lose control, lose himself. Sex—the twice she had tried it before—had never been the joyous, all-consuming, wildly amazing adventure that it was with Luke. She'd never realised what she had missed, had been so careful to never lose control, to never give anyone else a hold on her or power over her again, not after her mother, or her coach. She didn't want to need anyone. Luke understood that. At least, she thought he did. Now he wanted to change the rules, to change the whole basis of their relationship.

He had made it clear what he wanted from her—she just wasn't at all sure she could give it. Confused and troubled, she changed her clothes and then went through to the staffroom that served the radiology and orthopaedic departments to make herself a cup of coffee while she waited. She wasn't sure what she was going to say to Luke, she just needed to see him, to reassure herself they were still friends, whatever else happened.

The staffroom was empty when she went in. The coffee-jar was empty, too, so she went into the galley alcove that served as a store to find some more. She was out of sight in there when the staffroom door opened and several people came in, laughing and joking.

'You won't believe it but rumour is that Luke Devlin bagged the Ice Maiden this weekend,' one male voice she recognised as that of one of the junior doctors on the orthopaedic team announced.

Francesca froze, clutching the new full jar of coffee to her chest and staying hidden as the all-male conversation continued.

'No way!'

'Yeah.'

'I have a book running on it,' another voice chimed in. 'Want to place a bet?'

'Sure. Here's my stake. I say Devlin didn't get past first base.'

Several people laughed and then she heard the door open again.

'Here he is now,' the main instigator said. 'We can ask him. Hey, Luke, give us the details, man, I have a lot of money riding on you.'

Francesca pressed a hand to her mouth and fought back anger and pain. She felt used, humiliated, unable to believe that Luke would betray her. She had trusted him, had listened to his words that had seemed so sincere. Surely it couldn't all have been a joke, a bet?

'What are you talking about?' she heard Luke say.

'Is it true you thawed the Ice Maiden for us over the weekend?'

The room went quiet.

'What did you say?' Francesca could hear the chilling malice in Luke's voice.

She heard a grunt of surprise and another man called out, 'Luke! Easy, man. Come on, she's not worth it.'

What sounded like a fist meeting flesh echoed in the air.

'Damn you anyway, Devlin. I'll have you charged, I'll—'

'Shut the hell up.' She had never heard Luke so angry. 'If any one of you ever disrespects Francesca again, you'll find out firsthand how much of the Devlin blood I have in me. Do I make myself clear? And give me that money. You disgust me.'

'What are you going to do?'

'I'm going to give it to charity, where it might do some good for someone deserving rather than lining the pockets of cowardly scum like you.'

'Look, I'm sorry, man. I didn't realise you cared about her.'

'You have no idea. I've known Francesca nearly all my life. Aside from my mother, she is the only person who ever believed in me. Yeah, I care for her. More than care. I love her, I always have, and you have no idea what an amazing woman she is, what she has overcome, what an incredible person she is. All you can do is see the surface front she wears for protection and mock. That's your loss. If nothing else you owe her professional respect for the incredible job she does here.'

'Sounds like you're going to marry her or something.'

'I'd do it in a heartbeat if she'd have me. Whatever makes her happy. Francesca deserves the best of everything and if I had my wish I'd be there every day and every night to make sure she was cherished.'

Amazement welled inside her at Luke's words. The truth in them, the emotion and sincerity mirrored all he had said—and the way he had said it—the previous afternoon. Only hearing it now, in the way he defended her and declared himself to a group of their colleagues with no knowledge she was there, somehow set something free inside her. Something that dared to begin to believe.

She stepped out of the galley and surveyed the scene. Luke had his back to her. One guy was sitting on the floor holding a tissue to his bloodied nose, his partners in crime gathered around him.

Francesca cleared her throat.

All gazes swung to her. It was gratifying to see the shame and apology on the faces of her detractors. Then Luke turned round, as if in slow motion, and she saw no one else.

'Chessie. My God…' His voice was raw, his horror at seeing her there obvious in the shocked, pained expression in his green eyes.

Before she or anyone else had a chance to speak, however, the door opened yet again.

'What the hell is going on in here?' a voice boomed.

Everyone turned once more to stare at Maurice Goodwin, who stood, surveying the scene, Francesca's immediate superior Dee Miller and one of the hospital administrators by his side. Maurice took one look at the junior doctor with the bloodied nose and one look at Luke and ordered them all to his office. The room cleared quickly, before Francesca had a chance to say anything to Luke or defend him to his boss.

'Are you all right, Francesca?' Dee asked, her concern apparent.

'I'm fine,' she lied, masking how shaken she had been by what had happened. She turned to set the jar of coffee aside, then spotted a notebook on the floor. 'What's this?'

Bending to pick it up, she found it was the evidence of the junior doctors' bets on her—and other members of staff.

'You take that along to Maurice's office,' Dee

advised when she realised what it was. Smiling, her surperior held the door open for her. 'You might also like to know that Olivia Barr has been reported for her interference with patients—the Mitchells were not the only ones who complained about her. I doubt she'll avoid an official warning for her behaviour this time.'

'Thank you, Dee.'

'No problem, doll. Off you go, now, and remember how much we all value and respect you.'

Although grateful for the support and pleased about the news on Olivia, Francesca hurried out, Luke at the forefront of her mind. Filled with a sense of determination, and of déjà vu, she hurried to Maurice Goodwin's office.

Ignoring the scary-looking secretary who forbade her to go in, Francesca marched on, knocked once and opened the door before anyone could stop her. She didn't dare look at Luke who stood before the desk with the junior doctors in a row beside him. Instead, she focused on Maurice, who sat in his chair, the hospital administrator nearby. Walking forward, she handed the senior orthopaedic consultant the book.

'I think you'll recognise the writing, sir,' she

said, cursing the nervous wobble in her voice. 'Luke was kindly defending me from gossip about my private life and the insulting bets that were being placed on me by some of the staff. I thought you should know.'

'I'll speak with you outside, Francesca.'

Maurice rose to his feet and escorted her out of the door.

'Please, sir, it wasn't Luke's fault,' she tried again once they were alone. 'I know what some people call me around here and I just want to do my job. Luke was standing up for my professional reputation.'

'Yes, I understand that. Not that I approve of his methods, but I'll take your views into account.'

'Thank you.'

A smile stripped the sternness from the older man's face. 'Don't look so worried. I'm more angry at the despicable behaviour of the junior doctors,' he assured her, waving the book containing names and bets. 'Neither I nor the hospital administration will tolerate this kind of thing. You are a highly respected colleague, Francesca, and don't let a few thoughtless idiots give you cause to believe otherwise.'

'But Luke—'

'Trust me, my dear, I'm not so blind that I can't see how you feel about each other.' To her astonishment, the distinguished consultant winked at her. 'You go home and forget all about this unfortunate event. I'll bluster a bit, but this is not going to have a detrimental effect on Luke's career, I can promise you that.'

A smile on her own face, Francesca watched the man return to his office and close the door. Part of her wanted to wait, but she did as Mr Goodwin had advised and left the hospital. Instead of going straight home, however, she followed another, stronger instinct and headed for Annie's house. Her friend was home from her holiday in Italy and Francesca, who had never confided in anyone but Luke before, had a desperate need to seek her friend's advice.

Luke stifled a groan as his boss came back into the office alone, tapping the notebook against his hand. He looked stern, grim, but all Luke cared about was Francesca. He'd had no chance to explain, no opportunity to talk to her and reassure her that he'd had no idea what the young idiots had been doing. All he could see was the look of horror and humiliation on her face in the staffroom.

A shiver rippled through him and he recalled how similar this situation was to the time they had parted ten years ago—him being marched off to the headmaster's office to be told off for kissing her and Francesca storming along behind to defend him. Was that what she had done today? Had she believed in him, trusted that he hadn't betrayed her?

He soon learned that she had. But not before a dressing-down from Maurice and a lecture reminding that that using his fists was not the way to settle things. The junior doctors involved had a far rougher time, especially as Francesca had found the book and the evidence of names and what had been going on was there in black and white.

When he finally left his boss's office, daring to hope that maybe Francesca believed in him still, it was to find she had left the hospital. When she wasn't at home and wouldn't answer her mobile phone, he began to worry again. And worry led him to visit his mother, where he unloaded the whole story of the mess he had made of things.

'I wouldn't write Francesca off just yet,' she advised, pouring him a welcome cup of coffee.

'She has a sensible head on her shoulders. Give her some time and have a bit of faith. You look exhausted. You need to rest as you have another night shift ahead of you.' She laid a hand against his cheek. 'And don't you have a job you are meant to do this morning?'

Memory returned and he checked the clock. 'Thanks, Ma, I'd all but forgotten with everything else happening,' he admitted, finishing his coffee.

'You get off, now. Then go home and get some sleep. Things won't look so bad—trust in Francesca as you want her to trust in you.'

With his mother's advice ringing in his ears, he set off to keep his appointment and then went home. There was still no answer from Francesca's phone. He fretted for several moments and then decided against leaving her a text message. Doubts continued to gnaw at him. What if she said no—not to friendship but to commitment, the commitment he needed to keep his heart and soul together? He didn't know what he would do. He had promised not to leave, not to abandon her or withdraw his friendship, but how could he go on, loving her as he did, if she wanted nothing more? Cell by cell he would whither away.

Tired as he was, nothing was making sense, but the last place he wanted to go was to the bed he had last shared with Francesca just twenty-four hours ago. Everywhere held memories of her so there was no peace inside or outside the cottage. There was nothing else to do but wait it out and hope. His mother was right—as hard as it was, he had to trust that she would give him a chance—give *them* a chance.

If she didn't, then he would have lost the most important battle of his life—claiming Francesca and her love.

CHAPTER TEN

FRANCESCA hovered outside Annie and Nathan's house, wondering if she was doing the right thing.

'Are you going to stand there all day or are you going to come in?' Annie's voice made her jump and she looked up to see her friend lounging in the doorway. 'I saw you pacing about out here and thought I'd better grab you before you decided to leave without seeing me.'

It was so close to the truth that Francesca had to smile. She walked up the path to the front steps, delighted to see Annie looking so healthy. She was tanned and glowing, and she had put back on some of the weight she had lost during the ordeal of her trauma.

'You look amazing,' she praised truthfully.

'Thanks. I feel it. We had a brilliant time.' Annie took her by the arm and led her inside.

'You, on the other hand, are looking under the weather. Are you OK?'

Francesca shrugged, unsure now she was there what to say and where to start. As if sensing her discomfort, Annie took her through to the kitchen and set about making coffee, chatting about her and Nathan's visit to the villa on Elba.

'It was the most beautiful place ever,' she enthused with a blissful smile. 'I can see why Seb and his family love it so much—and why he and Gina are going to honeymoon there next month. Of course, the whole romantic fairy-tale story of Gina's grandparents adds to the mystique.' Pouring two mugs of coffee, she set them on the small table and they both sat down. 'Now it's back to reality, though. Nathan's gone back to work this morning. I'm getting fed up with convalescing, sitting around and doing nothing. And the place is so quiet now Will's moved out.'

A pout accompanied the news about Annie's irrepressible best friend and fellow A and E doctor Will Brown. 'I expect he felt a bit awkward with Nathan here and wanted to give the two of you time alone now you're on the mend,' Francesca suggested, knowing that

Nathan and Will had organised their shifts so that one of them was always home to care for Annie in the early days after she left hospital.

'I think it was more the lure of Anthony,' Annie corrected with a grin, her affection for and acceptance of Will's relationship with his firefighter boyfriend unmistakable.

'That could be it.' Francesca smiled back. 'So when is your next check-up?'

'At the end of the week. I hope to find out when I can start back at work, although I expect I'll have to do reduced hours to begin with,' Annie confided, her frustration evident.

They chatted a bit about the hospital and Gina's wedding arrangements, but Francesca's thoughts kept straying to Luke and what had happened that day. She couldn't stop thinking of the weekend either, and of his admission of his feelings for her.

'You're not really with me at all, are you?' Annie chuckled, clearly not put out.

'I'm sorry.'

'Don't be.' Her friend took a sip of her coffee. 'I'm out of touch with everyone's shifts but it looks like you've had a long night. Or does your distraction have something to do with a certain young surgeon?'

Francesca stared at her in amazement. 'You know about Luke?'

'Of course!'

'But how?'

Annie's blue eyes twinkled. 'Luke rang Nathan the day his mother broke her arm, wanting an update on the injury, and Nathan emailed him the X-ray images. Luke also talked about you. He asked if you were involved with anyone, and then if there were any orthopaedic vacancies here…which was good timing, given the hullabaloo of Adrian Lomax being sacked after the botched operation. So Nathan put Luke in touch with Maurice Goodwin. And then Luke confided to Nathan that he was coming back here for you.'

'He did? You never told me,' she accused, more surprised than put out.

'I didn't say anything because I know how you value your privacy and I respect that.' Annie's smile turned rueful as she continued. 'Besides, I'd made a bit of a mess of my own situation with Nathan, so I thought it best to keep out of it and let nature take its course with you and Luke.' She paused a moment her gaze assessing. 'I take it you have some things to think about.'

'You can say that again.'

Accepting another cup of coffee, Francesca started to explain the situation to Annie. She felt hesitant at first, unused to sharing confidences, but she found the more she talked, the easier it became, and soon she was telling her friend about the way she had grown up, her athletics, her mother's obsessive regime and how lonely she had been. She told her about Luke and how they had gravitated together, having very different backgrounds but both loners, both on the outside, and how Luke had looked out for her. Until he had left and she had truly felt lost.

There was more, and it all poured out, including what it had been like to see Luke again after ten years, that the closeness was still there but how her past held her back from giving up control of herself and her life, of committing to anyone. She told Annie about Olivia and the likelihood that the bitchy trauma nurse was in line for an official warning at last. And then she spoke about the events of the morning, about Luke's defence of her—again—and his declaration of love.

'Wow. It's about time Olivia got what was coming to her. And I hope those juniors get the ear-bashing they deserve.' Annie sighed and rested her arms on the table. 'As for your Luke, I can't wait to meet him. He sounds wonderful.'

That was irrefutable. 'Yes, he is.' Wonderful in so many ways, Francesca admitted to herself.

'So what's the problem?' her friend asked, getting to the heart of the matter.

Francesca paused, trying to gather together her jumbled thoughts and feelings. 'I don't know if I can commit. And the insecure part of me questions whether I deserve to be happy,' she admitted, acknowledging to herself her yearning for security, for self-determination. She also realised that her decision not to need anyone but herself was a protective mechanism to avoid getting hurt again.

'Of course you deserve to be happy. We all have a need to be loved, Francesca, and we all have doubts when we take that risk.'

'I just don't know if I can trust it. Or myself.' She sucked in a shaky breath. 'Luke was the only person I ever really cared about and when he left all those years ago, I felt so vulnerable.'

'But he came back,' Annie pointed out.

Yes, he had. Once to look for her when she had already been gone and again now, when he had uprooted his whole life for her. 'How do I know he won't leave again?'

'That's hardly likely, is it?' Annie refuted patiently. 'Luke gave up everything to come back as soon as his mother told him you were here. Everything he wants is in Strathlochan. It sounds to me that wherever you are, Luke will be there, too.'

Francesca thought of all Luke had done for her. He'd turned his back on a bright future in London. Working with the eminent Professor James Fielding-Smythe would have done wonders for his career and yet he had left all that to rush back to find her without a second thought. He had even bought her dream cottage, keeping hope alive at a point when there had seemingly been none. All for her. Not knowing if he would ever see her again and, if he did, whether she would ever be able to give him anything back but friendship.

Annie, who had listened in silence throughout, shook her head. 'He sounds pretty special to me.'

'I know.' Francesca sighed, not knowing how to explain. 'I've been alone so long, Annie, expected that I would always be alone. I guess this has thrown me off balance and I don't know how to let down my guard or relax my independence. I'm scared of getting hurt again and ending up being weaker.'

'All I can tell you, Francesca, is that being with Nathan makes me feel stronger, not weaker,' Annie told her. 'I've not lost anything of myself by being with him. Quite the opposite, in fact. I feel even more complete.'

It was true that Annie was an independent, successful woman and, despite her weeks of convalescence after being stabbed, she was still as lively and outgoing as before. But Nathan had definitely brought out an extra sparkle and confidence in her.

'And look at Callie,' Annie continued, warming to her theme. 'We both know about her terrible background in foster-care, her brief marriage to that horrible man, and then her cancer scare. Do you remember what she was like when she first came to Strathlochan?'

'Yes…Miss Feisty and Independent.' Francesca smiled at the memory of the girl with attitude their friend had been back then.

'Callie was so alone, so friendless, so untrusting, determined she would never need anyone. Yet with Frazer she has blossomed and mellowed. She is no longer fighting a lonely fight against the world. In many ways she's even stronger now than before. She's happy, contented, just as competent and independent and sure of what she wants, yet with a whole new added dimension to her life because of being with Frazer.'

Again, Francesca had to agree. In some cases, with the right person, it could work. Could it work for her? She wouldn't know unless she tried. But if it went wrong, if she lost Luke's friendship… She didn't realise she had spoken her fears aloud until Annie rested a hand on her arm, her eyes reflecting warmth and understanding.

'But what if you *don't* lose, Francesca? What if you gain so much more? Luke cares about you, and you clearly care about him. It sounds as if you have an incredible history. And you understand each other.' Annie paused a moment and then changed tack. 'Has Luke ever asked you to give up anything? Has he ever wanted you to be different? Has he ever tried to change you, to control you?'

'No.' On the contrary, Luke had always been supportive, her rock, defending her, encouraging her, helping her grow rather than cutting her down or holding her back. But the thought of opening herself up, of maybe losing what she already had, troubled her. 'It's scary, Annie.'

'Yes, but it's good scary. Exciting. An adrenalin rush. Like the best ride in the fair or the wildest white-water rafting. Not bad scary like a real fear of something terrible.'

Luke certainly gave *her* an adrenalin rush, Francesca thought. Being with him was exciting and beyond description. Annie was right, it *was* a real buzz. And besides Annie and Nathan, she could look at her other friends here in Strathlochan as examples. They had already spoken of Callie and Frazer. Then there were Ginger and Cameron, and not forgetting Gina who was getting married to Seb, her sexy and devoted Italian, in a few weeks' time. All successful women, who seemed to have grown even more since finding love with their one special man.

'What it comes down to, Francesca, is this,' Annie advised, breaking into her thoughts. 'Do you want life with Luke…or life without him?'

It was the choice she had given herself the afternoon before. And, when looked at that starkly, there really wasn't any choice at all. She began to understand. She wasn't losing herself by committing to Luke. Neither was she losing control. She was gaining it. They balanced each other. No one else knew or understood her as Luke did. No one else could make her feel the way he did. Out of control but safe in his hands, his heart, soaring free. He gave her that gift, made her feel whole. And he trusted her to do the same for him.

She *could* live without him. For ten years she had proved she could take care of herself and be successful…but she hadn't been happy, not deep inside. She could continue to walk alone and be strong. If she had to. Now, instead, she could contemplate sharing life and love with Luke as equals, making them both stronger still, complementing, enhancing, supporting each other, living in full colour rather than shades of grey.

Finally, she understood. She truly got what Luke meant and why this issue was so important to him…to them. If he was going to commit wholeheartedly to her in every way, then she had to trust him enough to commit the same to him. To know he loved her enough not to control and use her but to be her partner, working with her, not against her. Her very first instinct when she had seen him again after ten years had been to walk straight into his arms. Surely that told her something.

This last weekend had opened her eyes to what she could have with Luke. Aside from the friendship, trust and respect they shared, their mutual desire was indisputable, their sexual compatability red hot. And some, she admitted with a smile, feeling a charge of heat and want flow through her as she thought of the hours of amazing sex she had experienced with Luke. No. Not sex. Love-making. Luke had taught her the difference. And what an indescribable difference it was.

Everything came back to Luke, the one person who knew her totally, the good and the bad, and loved her anyway. The person she had trusted all her life without ever understanding why. The person with whom she could be herself, be accepted and be loved for who and what she was. The person she could laugh with, talk with, be silent with, be there to support and be supported by through the good times and the bad. The man who was her friend and her lover…her past, her present and her future.

A new sense of peace and rightness settled inside her. She knew now what she had to do. It was time to step off that cliff, to grasp what she most wanted, and to trust Luke to catch her and hold her tight.

Filled with new determination, she rose to her feet. 'Thanks, Annie.'

'Yes! Go get him, girl.' Her friend walked her to the door and gave her a hug. 'I take it you and Luke are on the same shifts?' Annie asked, and Francesca nodded. 'Well, when you come up for air on your next days off, I want to meet the wonderful man who has put such a special light in your eyes.'

Francesca hurried back to the hospital, her new sense of purpose faltering slightly when she discovered that Luke's car was no longer in its parking place. She deflated even more when she rushed home and discovered no message on her answering-machine. A check of her mobile found no text awaiting her either. As well as being anxious about what had happened to Luke in Maurice Goodwin's office in the aftermath of the row with the junior doctors and their bets, doubts started to play tricks on her mind. She could either sit at home and fret like some spineless damsel, or she could act like a gutsy modern woman and go and get her man.

Her first port of call was Luke's mother. She

leaned her bicycle against the wall outside the town house and rang the bell, her heart thudding in her chest, nerves clenching her stomach. There was no sign of Luke's car there either, so she presumed he had already gone home, but she decided she wanted, needed, to see Sadie.

The front door opened and the plump, kindly woman greeted her with a warm smile. 'Francesca! Come on in, lass. How lovely to see you.'

'Thank you.'

Adrenalin from the events of the morning had so far prevented the tiredness after a long and busy night shift from catching up with her. She politely declined more coffee, having drunk two cups at Annie's, but she was tempted by some of Sadie's delicious home baking, this time some fresh oatcakes spread with honey.

'I was looking for Luke,' she admitted after a few moments, feeling awkward. 'Have you seen him?'

'He stopped in earlier. I gather there was some bother at the hospital this morning,' Sadie responded with an understanding smile, gathering up Freya and giving the purring cat a cuddle.

Francesca nodded, unsure how much this

woman knew. Sadie was pretty shrewd. 'Did Luke get into trouble? Was everything all right?'

'He's fine. I'm sure he will tell you all about it himself. He had a couple of chores to run but I expect he's home by now.'

'Then he's probably asleep.' Francesca tried to smile to hide her disappointment. 'I'll catch up with him at work tonight.'

Sadie's own smile was full of affection and amusement. 'I think Luke would much rather see you now—even if that means you waking him up.'

'Oh…'

A gentle hand rested against her cheek. 'I believe things happen for a reason. Breaking my arm was meant to be because it led me to you and you brought Luke home,' the older woman said, startling her. 'I always wished I could have done more years ago to have made life easier for you as a child.'

'I think you had enough to contend with,' Francesca offered.

'Maybe. But I hated to see you so cut off. I've always looked on you as the daughter I never had, Francesca.'

The words warmed Francesca and brought a sting of tears to her eyes when she thought back to her youth and her longing for this woman to be her real mother. 'And I often dreamed you were my mother. It made me feel better,' she admitted with a tremulous smile that brought an answering shimmer of moisture to Sadie's eyes.

'I've vowed not to interfere, but I have to tell you, Francesca, that I've always thought you and Luke belonged together. And if you decide being with him is right for you, nothing would make me happier than gaining you as part of my family.'

'Thank you.'

To know that Sadie had cared about her—that she *still* cared about her—filled Francesca with warmth and joy. She welcomed Sadie's hug, fighting back the emotion that threatened to spill over, pondering Sadie's belief that things happened for a reason and the events that had brought her and Luke back together. Knowing she had his mother's blessing just made her feel even more complete, even luckier and more blessed.

'Now,' Sadie said, pulling back and wiping her eyes, 'you go and sort things out with that son of mine.'

There was nothing Francesca wanted more, so

she set a fast pace as she cycled through the out-skirts of town and down the country lane towards Luke's cottage—the cottage he had bought because he had remembered it was her dream. She was more sure in her heart than she had ever been that what she was doing was right. For the first time she felt real peace, knowing what she really wanted, knowing what she should have known from the first…that she couldn't live without Luke.

Her heart skipped a beat when the cottage came into view. It was still her dream home and right now it contained the man she loved, had always loved. Luke's car was outside and her pulse was racing, anticipation nearly over-whelming her as she rang the front doorbell.

It was some time before he answered, and when he did, dressed only in a pair of unfastened jeans, his feet and chest bare, his dark blond hair tousled, it took a moment for her to stop staring and remember how to breathe.

'Hi.'

'Chessie.'

He sounded defensive and wary. It wasn't the greeting she had hoped for and her fragile con-fidence slipped. She heard muffled noises from inside the house and thought her heart might actually stop. 'I'm sorry, I didn't realise you weren't alone.'

'That's all right.' Something she couldn't recognise flashed in his green eyes. 'Would you mind going round the side and coming in the garden door?'

'OK,' she managed, so taken aback and numb that she did as he'd asked rather than jump back on her bicycle and get the hell out of there, as instinct demanded. Did Luke not want her here after all? Had she made a big mistake about everything?

Wondering what was going on, and what—or who—Luke was hiding, Francesca walked down the gravel path to the gate, pausing to wipe suddenly damp palms on her jeans before she opened the gate and stepped into the garden, closing the gate behind her. Nearly paralysed with nerves, she had only taken a few unsteady steps towards the back door of the cottage, uncertain what she would find, when two black blurs appeared from nowhere and barrelled into her, knocking her on her rear on the grass.

For a moment she couldn't believe her eyes and then she was buried under two over-enthusiastic Newfoundland dogs, both trying to welcome her at the same time, tongues lolling and tails wagging madly. In disbelief, she hugged Murphy and Harry, the realisation sinking in that they were *here*, in the considerable flesh, which meant Luke had to have been the one to rehome them. The man was full of surprises. Scarcely realising that she was crying with happiness, she tried to wrestle herself free so that she could find Luke and tell him what she had come to say, her stupid, groundless fears at what was going on and who he had in the house long forgotten, lost in the exuberance of her joy.

Uncertain why Francesca had come, and hardly daring to hope it might be for the reasons he dreamed of, Luke headed through the house in time to find her flat on the grass and being greeted by Murphy and Harry. He couldn't help laughing at the sight of her as she struggled to sit up and hug both huge dogs at once, tears sliding down her face as fast as her canine companions could lick them away.

'Come on, guys,' he complained, bringing them to order. 'I'd kind of like a turn at greeting Chessie myself.'

It took a few moments, but he finally had the woman he loved back on her feet and, best of all, in his arms.

'You homed them!' she cried, laughing through her tears.

'I fell for them and would have taken them anyway,' he told her, restoring some order to her rumpled clothes and the wayward shambles of her fiery curls. 'But I did it for you. For us. What I hoped would be the start of our family.'

She hugged him tight. 'Oh, Luke.'

For a few moments he just held her, Murphy and Harry dancing around them. 'I couldn't find you at the hospital,' he murmured, breathing in her flowery fragrance, hearing the edge of worry and uncertainty in his own voice.

'I went to Annie's. I needed to think.' She paused, drawing back to look at him through grey eyes misted with tears. 'Then I saw your mother.'

Luke held his breath, recognising a new inner calmness radiating from her and hardly daring to believe it might mean what he thought it did…what he wanted it to. As impatient as he was, he forced himself to keep outwardly calm, although his heart was thudding and his stomach felt knotted with tension, and he kept silent, giving her time and space to speak. But he couldn't stop touching her, and while he waited, one hand stroked the silken mass of her hair while the fingertips of his other hand found the gap between the waistband of her jeans and the hem of her top and slowly carressed her soft, warm skin.

'I'm not at all sure I deserve you.' When he opened his mouth to protest, she pressed her fingers to his lips, cutting off his words. 'But,' she continued, her voice throaty from emotion and her tears, 'I hope to spend the rest of my life trying to prove that I do…loving you, supporting you, being your partner in everything and in every way, just as you have always been for me.'

His breath rushed out in a sigh of relief, and his heart swelled until he thought it would burst. 'Chessie…'

'I love you, Luke. I always have. I'm sorry it took me so long to see, to understand. But I'm here now—if you want me.'

'Of course I want you, you idiot woman!' he exclaimed with amused and loving exasperation, his mind already filling with his oft-dreamed-of image of half a dozen mini-Chessies with flame-red hair, freckles and silver-grey eyes.

He had wanted her admission that she needed

him as much as he needed her, wanted her acknowledgement and understanding that what they had was a partnership, that it was about sharing, about not only friendship but trust and love, too. Now he finally had what he'd so desperately wished for…Francesca's total commitment.

He wanted her in all the ways there were, would never get enough of her, was determined never to let her go and never to let her down. Somehow he had managed to break down her barriers, to cut through the reserve that kept her from giving of herself. Francesca now realised that being together could make the whole more than the sum of the separate parts, that together they could do anything.

The amethyst ring he had bought her sat in its box in a desk drawer in his study. One day he would slide it on her finger, sealing their promise to each other. But he was in no hurry to rush her to that, not now he had her heart. Life would always be different and special with Francesca. When the time was right, they'd likely go and get married on a beach somewhere, just the two of them. Whatever she wanted was fine with him.

Just the two of them…the way it had been in

the past and would now be for the rest of their lives from this point on. And that was all that mattered to him. What they had was special, unique. She belonged to him as he belonged to her…for ever.

'I'll spend the next fifty or sixty years loving you as I've always yearned to and as you deserve to be loved,' he promised her, the emotion of the moment affecting him. 'Starting now.'

She held him off as he moved in to kiss her. 'I'm covered in dog slobber and my bum's wet from sitting on the rain-soaked grass,' she complained with a mock pout, love and laughter shining in her eyes. 'And I need sleep—we have another night shift ahead of us.'

'Then I'd better take you indoors for a shower and put you to bed.'

'Mmm,' she responded, a naughty grin forming at his offer. 'Yes, please.'

Needing no further encouragement, Luke swung her into his arms and strode towards the cottage. As Murphy and Harry settled on their beds by the kitchen range, he carried Francesca to the bedroom. He had plans for her…plans that would last a lifetime.

* * *

There was nowhere else on earth she'd rather be than in Luke's arms. Smiling through her tears, she clung to his shoulders, burying her face against his neck, breathing in his masculine scent and tasting his skin with her tongue.

He set her down, the fire of desire in his green eyes as he slowly stripped off her clothes while she set to work on his jeans. And then they were under the spray of the shower and she was locked in his familiar embrace, meeting and matching the heady passion of his kiss. It was like coming home. Where she belonged.

As their bodies came together in urgent fulfilment and expression of their promises to and love for each other, Francesca knew that Luke needed her as much as she needed him. They were meant to be together. They always had been.

Now—finally—after all they had each been through growing up, and after ten years apart, they had found each other again. This was *their* time.

Luke had claimed her. Claimed her heart, her soul and her very being, as she had claimed his. The past was gone and ahead lay the future, one they would spend together, as one unit, stronger and safer, and secure in their love… for ever.

MEDICAL™

Large Print

Titles for the next six months...

January

THE VALTIERI MARRIAGE DEAL	Caroline Anderson
THE REBEL AND THE BABY DOCTOR	Joanna Neil
THE COUNTRY DOCTOR'S DAUGHTER	Gill Sanderson
SURGEON BOSS, BACHELOR DAD	Lucy Clark
THE GREEK DOCTOR'S PROPOSAL	Molly Evans
SINGLE FATHER: WIFE AND MOTHER WANTED	Sharon Archer

February

EMERGENCY: WIFE LOST AND FOUND	Carol Marinelli
A SPECIAL KIND OF FAMILY	Marion Lennox
HOT-SHOT SURGEON, CINDERELLA BRIDE	Alison Roberts
A SUMMER WEDDING AT WILLOWMERE	Abigail Gordon
MIRACLE: TWIN BABIES	Fiona Lowe
THE PLAYBOY DOCTOR CLAIMS HIS BRIDE	Janice Lynn

March

SECRET SHEIKH, SECRET BABY	Carol Marinelli
PREGNANT MIDWIFE: FATHER NEEDED	Fiona McArthur
HIS BABY BOMBSHELL	Jessica Matthews
FOUND: A MOTHER FOR HIS SON	Dianne Drake
THE PLAYBOY DOCTOR'S SURPRISE PROPOSAL	Anne Fraser
HIRED: GP AND WIFE	Judy Campbell

MEDICAL™

Large Print

April

ITALIAN DOCTOR, DREAM PROPOSAL	Margaret McDonagh
WANTED: A FATHER FOR HER TWINS	Emily Forbes
BRIDE ON THE CHILDREN'S WARD	Lucy Clark
MARRIAGE REUNITED: BABY ON THE WAY	Sharon Archer
THE REBEL OF PENHALLY BAY	Caroline Anderson
MARRYING THE PLAYBOY DOCTOR	Laura Iding

May

COUNTRY MIDWIFE, CHRISTMAS BRIDE	Abigail Gordon
GREEK DOCTOR: ONE MAGICAL CHRISTMAS	Meredith Webber
HER BABY OUT OF THE BLUE	Alison Roberts
A DOCTOR, A NURSE: A CHRISTMAS BABY	Amy Andrews
SPANISH DOCTOR, PREGNANT MIDWIFE	Anne Fraser
EXPECTING A CHRISTMAS MIRACLE	Laura Iding

June

SNOWBOUND: MIRACLE MARRIAGE	Sarah Morgan
CHRISTMAS EVE: DOORSTEP DELIVERY	Sarah Morgan
HOT-SHOT DOC, CHRISTMAS BRIDE	Joanna Neil
CHRISTMAS AT RIVERCUT MANOR	Gill Sanderson
FALLING FOR THE PLAYBOY MILLIONAIRE	Kate Hardy
THE SURGEON'S NEW-YEAR WEDDING WISH	Laura Iding

™ MILLS & BOON®

millsandboon.co.uk Community

Join Us!

The Community is the perfect place to meet and chat to kindred spirits who love books and reading as much as you do, but it's also the place to:

- **Get the inside scoop from authors about their latest books**
- **Learn how to write a romance book with advice from our editors**
- **Help us to continue publishing the best in women's fiction**
- **Share your thoughts on the books we publish**
- **Befriend other users**

Forums: Interact with each other as well as authors, editors and a whole host of other users worldwide.

Blogs: Every registered community member has their own blog to tell the world what they're up to and what's on their mind.

Book Challenge: We're aiming to read 5,000 books and have joined forces with The Reading Agency in our inaugural Book Challenge.

Profile Page: Showcase yourself and keep a record of your recent community activity.

Social Networking: We've added buttons at the end of every post to share via digg, Facebook, Google, Yahoo, technorati and de.licio.us.

www.millsandboon.co.uk